Harry Harrison was born in Stamford, Connecticut in 1925 and lived in New York City until 1943, when he joined the United States Ar~~my~~  during the war, but retu~~rned~~ e army. A career first as a~~n~~ director and edit~~or~~ magazines fitted ~~him~~ ew York, so he changed it f~~or~~ xistence and moved his family to Cuautla, Mexico. Since then he has lived in Kent, Camden, Italy, Denmark, Spain and Surrey; he has now returned to his native land, but he has not ceased to wander. He rationalizes this continual change of residence as essential research, when in reality it is an incurable case of wanderlust that enables him to indulge all his enthusiasms: travel, skiing, practising Esperanto, and making an annual pilgrimage to the Easter Congress of the British Science Fiction Association.

Harry Harrison

Star Smashers of the Galaxy Rangers

Futura Publications Limited
An Orbit Book

An Orbit Book

First published in Great Britain in 1974
by Faber and Faber Limited

First Orbit edition 1976
published by Futura Publications Ltd
Reprinted 1977

ISBN 0 8600 7850 7

Printed in Great Britain by
Hazell Watson & Viney Ltd,
Aylesbury, Bucks

To the onlie believers
B.W.A., J.B., L.E.S.

Futura Publications Limited
Warner Road, London SE5

JEST 89,000 VOLTS

"Come on, Jerry," Chuck called out cheerfully from inside the rude shed that the two chums had fixed up as a simple laboratory. "The old particle accelerator is fired up and rarin' to go!"

"I'm fired up and rarin' to go too," Jerry whispered into the delicate rose ear of lovely Sally Goodfellow, his lips smacking their way along her jaw towards her lips, his insidious hands stealthily encircling her waist.

"Silly!" Sally giggled and wriggled free of his powerful, yet tender embrace with a solid blow of the heel of her hand against his chin. "You know that I like Chuck just as much as I like you." Then, with a saucy toss of her shoulder-length locks she was gone, and Jerry looked after her longingly, fingering his bruised jaw.

"Come on, Jerry, the accumulators are crackling with barely restrained power," Chuck shouted.

"Here I come."

Jerry entered the shed and closed and locked the door carefully behind him, for there were discoveries and yet-unpatented inventions here that would set the largest corporations in the land to·licking their lips. It just so happened that these two young men, still students at a secluded State College in drowsy Pleasantville, had two of the keenest minds in the country, perhaps the entire world. Tall, dark-haired, broad-shouldered Jerry Courteney, handsome as a Greek god with a whimsical smile forever playing about his lips, would never be taken for the topnotch engineer that he was, the man who walked off with every medal and every award in every field that he chose to study. He looked less like a scholar than the rugged frontiersman he really was, for he had been born up on the far northern border of our country, on a homesteaded ranch in Alaska north of the Arctic Circle. In that rough environment he had grown up with his four strapping brothers and strapping father, who strapped them all quite well when they got out of line, as high-spirited boys ever will. The others were all still there, hewing a precarious living from the virgin wilderness, but much as he loved the icy silences and whispering trees, Jerry had been bitten by the bug of knowledge, just as his arms were bitten by the ravenous mosquitoes so his skin was tougher than shoe leather, and had made his way from school to school, scholarship to scholarship until he reached State College.

Chuck van Chider, no less of a genius, had had a far easier time of it. A blond giant of man with arms as thick as a strong man's legs, he was the heart and spirit of the State Stegasauri, the championship football team, the man who could open a hole in any line, who could carry the ball through any number of grappling foe. When he remembered to. Twice during the last season he had stopped stock still with the game surging around him as a solution to a complicated mathematical problem suddenly presented itself to him. He went on to win these games, so his teammates never minded the blank moments, and he was also the heir to the van Chider millions which also did not make him any enemies. Born with a platinum spoon in his mouth, his father had prospected a platinum mine on the very spot where the Pleasantville Mental Hospital now stood; he had never known want. Before the mine had played out, the shrewd Chester van Chider had sold out and used the money to buy the tiny cheese works outside of town. By the addition of inert ingredients and deliquescing agents to the sturdy cheese he had built a world wide market for Van Chider Cheddar—and a fortune for himself. Though discontented radicals from the lunatic fringe often said his cheese tasted like rancid sealing wax, the public at large loved it, mostly for its deliquescing agents which absorbed water from the atmosphere so that after a few days, if you didn't eat fast enough, you had more cheese than you started with. Chester van Chider was a shrewd businessman, unlike the greedy operators who bought his platinum mine only to have it play out a few weeks later, this blow being so great that most of them ended up in the aforementioned looney bin built on the minesite. The keen business mind of the father was reflected in the mathematical genius of the son.

In some ways as different as night and day, blond and dark-haired, wiry and stocky, the two friends were very much alike inside. They had strong hearts and rugged digestions—and minds that were as keen as any that could be found. All around them, in the cluttered laboratory that had once been a simple shed, lay the fruits of their mutual genius. A tossed-aside bit of breadboard circuitry that would one day revolutionize long-line transmission of electricity, a bit of scribbled paper that elaborated a simple equation for squaring the circle. These were the playthings of their ever-curious minds—and their latest plaything now filled the room and hummed with life. A massive, hulking, 89,000-volt particle accelerator that they had put together from surplus electromagnets and a rusty water boiler. High-density batteries of their own invention brimmed full of electricity, and all that was required now was to throw the great gang switch to send the charged particles smashing into the target.

"Put the rubidium on the target area, will you?" Chuck called out, busily at work adjusting a meter, his thick, strong fingers as delicate as those of a master watchmaker at the precise job.

"Right on," Jerry answered and reached for the sample of the rare metal they were bombarding—but seized instead a piece of Van Chider Cheddar from the large wheel they always kept nearby. It was a moment of youthful madness, a harmless jest brought on perhaps by the still-warm memory of those precious lips against which his had so recently rested. Filled with the joy of life, he prized the damp piece of cheese free and slapped it onto the chamber and sealed and evacuated it.

"Stand clear," Chuck shouted. "There she blows!"

With a mighty crackling the batteries discharged com-

7

pletely, and the sharp smell of ozone filled the air. Visible only as a sudden fine beam of purple light, the particles struck the target and vanished.

"Experiment eighty-three," Chuck said, licking a pencil and making a note on the chart. The clamps pulled free and the cover came away and he looked in at the target and his eyes bulged and the pencil fell from his limp fingers. "I'll be double gosh-darned!" he whispered.

Jerry could contain himself no longer but burst out laughing at his friend's astonishment. "Just a joke," he gasped through the laughter. "I put some cheese in place of the rubidium."

"This is *cheese?*" Chuck asked, and withdrew a spherical black lump from the target area.

This time it was Jerry's turn to gape and gasp, and Chuck enjoyed a good chuckle at his friend's discomfiture. But the fun once over, they turned their attention to the sudden mystery.

"It was cheese before it was bombarded," Jerry said, suddenly serious, looking at the shiny black pellet through a strong lens.

"There are a number of unusual chemicals in my father's cheese. Somehow they united under the bombardment to form this new compound, once the large quantities of hydrogen and oxygen had been freed from the water. What can it be?"

"We can find out easily enough—but I have just had an idea. Take a vacuum tube. . . ."

"Of course, I had the same obvious idea. Put this new substance in place of the cathode and hook it up and see what kind of signal it produces."

"Exactly my idea." Jerry smiled. "But we need a name for this substance."

"I think cheddite fills the bill."

"Bang on!"

They cracked the glass casing of a hulking PF167 power tube and put the mysterious fragment of cheddite in place of the cathode, Jerry deftly wiring it into the circuit while Chuck took a glass rod and quickly blew a new envelope for the tube. A few moments more sufficed to wire

8

the tube into a breadboarded amplifier circuit and to switch the power on.

"Give it some more juice," Jerry said, frowning at the meters hooked up to the output of the circuit.

"She's taking all we have now," Chuck answered, spinning the great theostat to its final stop.

"Well, then there's something mighty fishy here. Look. The current is pouring into the circuit—but it is not coming out! Not a needle has flickered from the stops. Where is all that energy going?"

Chuck scratched his wide jaw in puzzlement. "It's not coming out as volts or ohms or watts, that is for sure. So it must be radiant energy of a different kind. Let's hook up a hunk of aerial to that output and see what kind of signal it is putting out."

A handy metal coat hanger served that function well and was wired into the circuit while test instruments were set up around it.

"I'll give it just a millivolt first," Jerry said as he threw the switch.

What happened next was as soundless as it was shocking. The moment the current went into the circuit *something* was broadcast from the coat hanger-aerial, because a coat-hanger-shaped chunk of wall instantly vanished. It happened soundlessly and in a fraction of a second of time. Jerry hurled off the current, and they rushed to the wall. Through the new opening they could see the board fence that circled the backyard—and the same strange force had also taken a coat-hanger-shaped section from the fence as well.

"And spreading," Chuck mused. "That hole in the fence is two or three times as big as the first opening."

"Not only that," Jerry said, squinting along the edge of the hole. "If you look, you'll see a stub of a mast next door where the Grays' new color TV aerial used to be. And, let me think for a second, yes, I'm right. That missing section of fence is where the landlady's cat sleeps in the afternoon. And he *was* sleeping there when I came in."

"This will take some thinking out," Chuck said as they hammered boards over the opening in the wall. "We had better keep it to ourselves for a while. I'll send an anonymous check to the Grays for their aerial."

"We better think about an anonymous cat for my landlady as well."

A sudden knocking on the door startled them both, and they exchanged glances, for it was the landlady calling to them. Mrs. Hosenpefer was a good woman, though advanced in years, a widow who had run her home as a boardinghouse ever since her husband, a switchman on the railroad, had met a tragic end under a boxcar that his advancing deafness had prevented hearing approach. Somewhat guiltily the two young men opened the door to face the white-haired widow wringing her hands with despair.

"I don't know what to do," she wailed, "and I know I shouldn't bother you out here, but something terrible has happened. My cat"—both listeners recoiled at the word—"has been stolen. Poor Max, who would do that to a sweet harmless animal like that?"

"Just what do you mean *stolen?*" Jerry asked, fighting desperately to keep the tension out of his voice.

"I can't imagine why, some people will do awful things these days, it must be the drugs. Here I thought my Max was asleep on the fence out there"—the two listening men stirred ever so slightly at the words—"but he wasn't. Kidnapped. I just had a phone call from the sheriff in Clarktown that somebody had thrown Max through a window or something right into the middle of the Unreformed Baptist choir practice. Max was very angry and scratched the soloist. They caught him and called me because of the tag on his collar."

"This call came through *now?*" Jerry asked, innocently.

"Not a minute ago. I rushed right out here to ask for help."

"And Clarktown is eighty miles away," Chuck said, and the chums exchanged pregnant, significant glances.

"I know, an awful distance. How can I get my darling Max back?"

"Now don't you worry an instant," Jerry said, gently ushering the bereaved woman out. "We'll drive right over and get Max. It's in the bag." The closing door shut off

10

her cries of gratitude, and the experimenters faced each other.

"Eighty miles!" Chuck shouted.

"Instantaneous transmission!"

"We've done it!"

"Done what?"

"I don't know—but whatever it is, I feel it is a great step forward for mankind!"

2

A SHOCKING DISCOVERY

"We'll just have to go back to the old drawing board." Chuck sighed gloomily, looking at the large hole in the ground where the boulder had been and at the larger hole in the nearby hillside. "We just can't control the cheddite projector no matter how hard we try."

"Let me have one more go," Jerry muttered as he probed the depths of the device with a long-shanked screwdriver. For security's sake they had built their invention into a small portable Japanese television set, and so cunningly contrived the inner wiring that it still functioned as a TV as well. Jerry finished his adjustment and switched the set on. There was a quick glimpse of a vampire sinking his fangs into a girl's fair neck before a secret button activated the cheddite projector. The TV screen now displayed a complex wave form which changed shape as further adjustments were made.

"I think this is it." Jerry grinned as he sighted along the aerial. "I'm going to focus on that stick and move it over by the ridge there. Here goes."

There was no sound or visible radiation from the device, but the cheddite force sprang out, unseen yet irresistible. The stick did not move. However, a great rock a hundred yards away disappeared in a fraction of a second and reappeared over the lake behind them. The sudden tumultuous splashing was followed instantly by a wave of water that washed around their ankles.

"Our problem is control." Chuck grimaced unhappily, wiping off the TV set.

"There has to be a way," Jerry said, his words as firm as the set of his jaw. "We know that the cheddite produces a wave of kappa radiation that drops anything in its field through into the lambda dimension where space time laws as we know them do not exist. It appears from the mathematical model you constructed that this lambda dimension, while congruent with ours in every way, is really very much smaller. What was your estimate?"

"Roughly, our spiral galaxy which is about eighty thousand light-years across is, in the lambda dimension, about a mile and a half wide."

"Right. So anything moving a short distance in the lambda dimension will have moved an incredible distance in our own dimension when it emerges. That's the theory all right, and it checks out to fifteen decimal places—but why can't we make it work?"

It was then that Jerry realized that he was talking to himself. Chuck had that glazed look in his eyes that meant his brain was churning away busily at some complex mathematical theorem. Jerry recognized the signs and smiled understandingly as he packed the cheddite projector and test equipment into the back of their battered jeep. He had just finished doing this when Chuck snapped back to reality as suddenly as he had left.

"I have it. Molecular interference."

"Of course!" Jerry said gleefully, snapping his fingers. "It's obvious. The kappa radiation is deflected ever so minutely by the atmosphere. No wonder we couldn't control the results. We'll have to carry on the rest of the experiments in a vacuum. But it will be some job to build a big vacuum chamber."

"There's one we can use not far away," Chuck said with a chuckle. "Just one hundred miles . . ."

They burst out laughing together as Jerry pointed straight up. "You're so right—there's all the vacuum we need up there. Just a matter of getting to it."

"The *Pleasantville Eagle* will take care of that. We'll say that we're testing, what? Navigational equipment. They'll let us borrow her."

The *Pleasantville Eagle* was the plane that flew the football team to all its games. Since it was a 747, it flew most of the spectators as well. Both Jerry and Chuck were trained pilots, as well as superb rifle shots and champion polo players, so had relieved the pilot at the controls many times. They had modified and improved most of the electronic equipment on the big plane so it seemed only natural that they would have improvements for the navigational rig as well. They would have no trouble getting permission to test fly the plane, none at all. Particularly since Chuck's dad had donated the plane to the school in the first place.

They hurried back to the lab and had just finished building the cheddite projector into a navigation frequency receiver when there came a familiar light tapping at the door. Both young men sprang to open it, scuffling good-naturedly before throwing it wide.

"Hi," Sally Goodfellow said cheerfully, strolling in casually, a vision in a green cotton summer frock, almost the same green as her lovely eyes, her shoulder-length hair the color of golden cornsilk. "What are you two guys up to now?"

"Same old stuff," Jerry said offhandedly as Chuck winked broadly behind the girl's back. No one, they had agreed, *no one* was to know about the cheddite projector until they had tested it thoroughly. They had taken their oath on that, and as much as they loved Sally with every fiber of their beings, they would not break that oath.

"What old stuff?" Sally asked, not deceived for an instant.

"Improved navigation aid. You're just in time to drive us to the field so we can install it on the *Eagle*. We have the jeep engine apart, rebuilding it."

Sally arched one delicate eyebrow. "You really think I'll buy this story about navigational aids? I know that is one thing your new invention is *not*. Remember how you told me the flying wing design was a kid's kite? And the paralysis vibrator was a soldering gun? So what do we *really* have here?"

Both of them had the good manners to blush, but in response to her questioning they only returned mumbled evasions and rushed to load the equipment into the back

14

seat of her yellow convertible. Seeing that frontal attack had failed, she decided on subtlety which worked well for her for she had a fine mind, almost as good as that of her father, Professor Goodfellow, the school president.

"Sit up here with me, Chuck," she said, patting the front seat invitingly. "Jerry can ride in back and look after your old equipment."

Chuck was only too eager to oblige, and they chatted happily all the way to the airport, driving into the glory of the summer sunset. Sally parked under the great wing of the *Pleasantville Eagle* so they could unload. Jerry saw Old John shuffling between the buildings with his trusty mop and pail and called him over to help them. Old John was an institution at this institution, a black gentleman of advanced years.

"Dat's some mighty heavy stuff you have dere. Too much for an old man like me." But there was a glint of unspoken humor in his eye as he bent to lift the hundred-pound transceiver in one hand. A lifetime of hard labor had made no weakling of him.

They made their way through the cavernous plane to the flight deck above the nose, where they set to work at once with their soldering irons while Sally watched with growing curiosity.

"Do you have the axis-traction forceps?" Jerry asked, half buried in the equipment. "I really need them to get at this baby."

"They're not here," Chuck answered after rooting through the tool box. "Maybe we left them in the car. I'll go look."

He made his way back through the now-darkened plane to the car and found the forceps where they had slid under the front seat. Whistling quietly through his teeth, he was making his way back through the gloom of the great cabin when a voice called to him.

"Chuck. Over here."

It was Sally, sitting by a window and beckoning him toward her, the last light of day touching her sweet profile with gold. He went over to her, and she smiled.

15

"There's something I want to show you," she said, and when he was close, she pulled forward the top of her scoopneck dress. "No bra," she husked.

Even in that dim light the blush that suffused Chuck's fair skin could be seen as a rising tide of scarlet. Yet, despite his shyness, his reflexes were still hard at work.

"Not until you tell me what the new invention is." Sally laughed saucily, slapping aside his questing wrist as she pushed shut the neck of her dress.

"Sally, honey, you know I can't, gee, we have an oath. . . ."

"I have something twice as good as an oath," she murmured, pulling her dress forward again. "See? The invention?"

"It's, well, hard to say." His voice was thick and turgid.

"You'll find a way." She guided his hand. "Here, this will help."

In an almost hypnotized voice Chuck began to talk. But, even as the first words left his mouth, he heard a tiny clinking sound and, his attention drawn now, was aware of a darker form in the darkness of the cabin. With great reluctance he drew away from Sally and turned on the light above the seat.

"Who's there?" he called out, clenching one great fist. "Come out."

There was a rustle a few rows down, and a familiar figure emerged.

"Just cleaning out the ashtrays, suh," Old John said. "Gotta be spick-'n-span for the next game."

They both laughed, and Chuck patted the old man on the shoulder. "Better go clean the trays in the aft section," he said kindly.

Old John ambled off, and Sally sat down again, Chuck dropping heavily beside her, and they were just getting back on the job where they had left off when the rasping of the loudspeakers caused them to jump up hurriedly.

"Chuck," Jerry's voice said. "Just about done up here. Bring that forceps on the double, and we'll see if this old thing really works."

16

There was repressed excitement in the tiny cabin as Jerry made the last connections.

"There," he said, leaning back and wiping his grease-stained hand on a piece of cloth. "Ready to go. All that has to be done is to take her up and try her out."

"Oh, please," Sally begged. "Please let me come with you. I know it is something exciting."

"Exciting isn't the word for it!" Jerry chortled. "This is the greatest ball of wax to ever come down the pike, you wait and see. Once we prove the theory tonight."

"The whole world will know by tomorrow when we break the news," Chuck said. "So why don't we tell Sally now? She's a good sport and won't spill the beans."

They nodded in silent agreement with each other.

"Why not?" Jerry grinned. "It is only something that will revolutionize transportation, that's all. I won't go into exactly how it works, it's a little complicated, and besides, it's a secret. But to put it simply the cheddite projector here will move this entire plane a couple of hundred miles in a fraction of a second, bang, just like that."

"What a saving on fuel!" Sally gasped.

"You're not just whistling 'Dixie'," Chuck agreed. "But more than just the saving in fuel will be the saving in time. With this gadget aboard, all a plane has to do is take off and hover over the airport, press the button, and *zing* they are over the other airport, maybe all the way across the country."

"It could be important for defense too," Jerry said, suddenly serious. "The Air Force will have to be the first to know."

"If it works," Chuck said, inserting a note of caution into the conversation. "But by tomorrow we will know for certain."

"For you," a guttural, husky voice, rich with menace, said, "there will be no tomorrow. I'm taking over."

As one they spun about and looked at the open doorway, their jaws dropping in unison. Old John stood there, but suddenly, as though a mask had been ripped away, they saw that Old John was not as old as they had

17

thought. Was that powder that turned his hair gray at the temples? He stood straighter, alert, a sneer slashed across his features.

A Russian 7.62mm Shpagin M1941 PKS submachine gun was cradled in his arms, the gaping, deadly mouth pointing unswervingly in their direction.

3

AN UNEXPECTED JOURNEY

Shocked, unbelieving silence filled the cabin like a gray fog. Chuck shook his head as though to clear it, for this situation was impossible. Sally spoke, gasping, speaking for them all.

"This is impossible!"

In response the sneer on Old John's features only widened, and he slapped the blue steel of the gun with one hand. "This is not only possible but it is a 7.62mm PKS capable of firing twenty-two shots a second—so put up your hands."

They raised their hands.

"Think of what you are doing," Jerry entreated, appealing to the man's higher senses. "You're throwing up a good salary, security, a fine pension soon, for what? For some desperate plan that cannot possibly work. Who paid you to do this—the Black Panthers?"

"I am far beyond your petty bourgeois internal disruptionary feuds," he sneered viciously, reaching into his pocket, while the gun barrel never wavered a fraction of an inch, and taking out a green cap which he pulled on at a jaunty angle over one eye. As his hand came away, they all gasped in unison for there, blazoned boldly on the front, was a great red star with the gold letters CCCP below it. He smiled coldly at their consternation. "You will now stop calling me by my cover name and will refer to me by my correct title of Lieutenant Johann Schwarzhandler of the Soviet Secret Police." As he said this, he clicked his heels together, the sound loud in the tiny cabin.

"You can't mean it." Chuck gaped. "You're no Russian. I mean you don't look like a Russian. I mean, you know, Russians, blond hair and cigarettes hanging from their lips. . . ."

"Prejudiced capitalist honky swine! You think that every black man in the world is a willing slave to his imperialist masters. You forget that there are parts of the world where the free air of socialism is breathed by the unshackled arms of workers freed from the repressive toils of the so-called free enterprise system. My father, who was born on One Hundred and Twenty-fifth Street in the city of New York, breathed that free air while reluctantly serving in your warmongering Army in Germany and married my mother, who was from the People's Democratic Republic of Germany, but enough, I waste my breath talking to you. Suffice to say that after my father's untimely death my mother returned to her ancestral home, and I grew to stalwart manhood under the snapping red flag of freedom."

"Treacherous turncoat Commie swine," Jerry murmured through clenched teeth.

"Flattery will get you nowhere. Now do as I say—"

Chuck stepped forward, mighty fists clenched, and the muzzle of the gun swung toward him. Instantly, Jerry dived for Johann. But the Soviet spy was too fast for him. He stepped back and swung the gun, and a single shot cracked out, booming loudly in the confined space. Jerry dropped, a growing red stain on his shirt, and Sally screamed.

"Do not move," their captor ordered. "You have no chance to escape, as I have just demonstrated, since I am a perfect shot. That single bullet penetrated Jerry's biceps, and you will find the spent slug lodged in the second volume of *American Airports* in the navigator's cubby. Now —about face and march out of here!"

They had no recourse but to obey. Sally wrapped her scarf around the neat hole drilled in Jerry's arm, and they walked reluctantly down the brightly illuminated corridor of the plane until they came to the toilet area.

"Far enough," the Soviet spy called out. "Each of you into one of the booths, and I want to see the *occupied* lights come on."

With dragging feet they followed the cruel instructions,

and Jerry had one last glimpse of Sally's endearing smile and the wave of a tiny hand before the prison door clanged shut behind her. Then Jerry entered his own cell and busied himself washing and cleaning his wound and binding it up again, gritting his teeth and ignoring the pain. Suddenly his sensitive nostrils twitched, and he jumped about. Yes! There was a glowing red light at the crack around the door, and the paint was beginning to blister. Muttering an oath under his breath, he unbolted the door and hurled his weight against it. It did not even quiver. The thud of his body and his groan as he realized he had hit the door with the wrong shoulder were echoed by sardonical laughter from the corridor outside.

"Yes," a wickedly jubilant voice called out, "The doors to your cells are welded shut, for I brought the oxyhydrogen torch with me that you so carefully provided. Now that you are secure I can tell you that not only am I an excellent shot, but I am also an experienced pilot with thousands of hours on aircraft of all kinds. You undoubtedly thought I would attempt to steal your invention and escape and that you would then track me down and recapture me." The silence that followed indicated the acuteness of this observation. "Well, you were wrong. I shall now fly this plane to Mother Russia, where experts will go over it inch by inch, and also over *you* inch by inch as well!"

His wild laughter sounded over the thud-thud of their helpless bodies bounding off the cruel steel of their cells. He knew that if he had told them earlier of his plan, they would have died fighting rather than be carried into foreign bondage. But now it was too late. The sound of Johann's retreating footsteps sounded the death knell to their hopes.

"It's all over then?" Sally sobbed, her voice clearly heard by the others through the thin but sturdy walls of their prison.

"Nothing is over until death draws the final curtain," Chuck said stoutly to cheer her up. "I'll put my mind to this." He instantly began thinking and lost contact with

21

the others no matter how loudly they shouted and banged on the wall. Jerry gritted his teeth and clenched his fists and ignored the pain that tore at his arm.

"I just don't know the word 'defeat'," he said grimly, and Sally took heart from his words and washed her tear-stained face, then sat on the john and put her makeup back on. She had faith in Jerry.

But Jerry was losing faith in himself. First one engine, then another started, until all four of the giants were rumbling with power and the great plane surged forward toward the runway. What could he do? He swept the limited environs of his cell with the eyes of a trapped animal. How could he escape? He realized then that a mixture of panic and pain was beginning to take over and that would not do. American grit was not defeated that easily. He took a deep breath and forced himself to *think*.

Two minutes of concentrated thought gave him the answer. By that time they were airborne, which was all for the good since the noise of the engines would cover any sounds he might make. He carefully emptied all money, rubbers and credit cards from his plastic wallet and with infinite patience and his pocketknife he cut the wallet into thin shreds in the stainless steel sink. He then added a specific amount of liquid soap and kneaded the resultant mixture to a doughy mass. Any ninth-year chemistry student could have figured this one out, and he marveled at his slowness in taking so long to think of it. These two innocent substances, plastic and soap, when mixed in the proper proportions and heated to the correct temperature —he held his cigarette lighter under the sink for exactly four minutes and twelve seconds—polymerized into a powerful explosive. It was ready! Working quickly, he pressed the plastic mixture into the doorjamb from roof to floor, where it instantly congealed. Then, getting a firm grip with his fingers and tensing his powerful muscles, he tore off the top of the monomatic toilet, exposing its innards. Rushing against time, he pulled out the length of wire that controlled its operation and pushed its bare copper ends into the now-stiffened plastic explosive.

"All or nothing," he said jauntily and pressed himself as

22

far back in the corner as he could and held a wad of wet paper towels before his face and, with forceful decision, pressed the switch to flush the toilet. The diverted current raced through the wires and into the plastic explosive. . . .

If there had been a watcher in the corridor, which there wasn't, he would have seen a crackling red explosion gout out from around the door, followed by a burst of smoke, followed by the door itself which flew into the chairs opposite. Followed by a ragged, smoke-stained and scorched, yet still jubilant figure that staggered to freedom clutching the wet paper towels.

"What was that?" Chuck called out, jarred from introspection by the explosion.

"The liberty bell," Jerry said and coughed out a lungful of smoke. "Let's just hope our Russky friend on the bridge didn't hear it. Now look at that—he was obliging enough to leave the torch here."

Moments later the doors were open and the three friends reunited. While the two men shook hands firmly and began planning their bid to retake control of the plane, the industrious Sally found a first-aid kit and put unguents on Jerry's burns and redressed the wound in his arm.

"Rush him and grab him," Chuck growled, his great fists clenching as though they already had the enemy neck in their grasp.

"He's too shrewd for that," Jerry disagreed. "He'd shoot us like clay pigeons before we got halfway to him. We need a better plan. Any shooting and someone gets hurt or the plane is wrecked. I have the feeling he would rather dive this thing into the ground than surrender."

"You're right. We need sound thought, not brutal violence, and that's my clue to put on the old thinking cap."

His eyes glazed in a familiar fashion, and Jerry, ever a man of action, ignored his burns and bruises and pulled Sally down into the seat next to him and got his arm around her and nibbled his way up her neck to her mouth and was putting all of him into a gustatory soul kiss when Chuck snapped his fingers and rejoined them, too carried

23

away by his new idea to notice the rapid pulling away, straightening of clothing and wiping of chins.

"Here it is, and it can't be stopped. You remember we set up the cheddite projector to work through the radar aerial on top of the plane, right?"

"Right!"

"Okay. So the field envelops the entire plane. What I am going to do—me, not you, Jerry, so don't argue, not with that busted wing—is sneak into the radio operator's cubby where we installed the equipment. Even if that Russky spots me, I can reach it before he can plug me. Then I'll have a couple of seconds before he can set the automatic pilot and come after me. Two seconds is all I need. I'll set the direction on a hundred and eighty degrees and give it a thousandth of a volt, and you know what that means."

Jerry's forehead puckered as he did some quick calculation. "As near as I can figure it, that will put the plane over the middle of Hudson's Bay in Canada."

"Right! There will be just enough fuel left by then to reach an airfield in Canada, but not enough to fly to Russia or Siberia or Cuba. We can play it by ear from there."

"A good plan, and the only chance we have. Let's go!"

The muttered roar of the great engines covered their approach as they crept stealthily through the first-class lounge toward the open door of the pilot's compartment. Through the opening they caught a quick glimpse of the hijacking spy's head as he sat at the controls, outlined against the star-filled sky beyond. Chuck shook hands quickly with his friends and smiled happily when Sally stood on tiptoe to give him a quick kiss. Then, with a wry wave of his hand, he began creeping forward.

He had almost reached the door to the radioman's cubby when something disturbed Johann, some noise heard or perhaps a spy's highly developed sixth sense. At first he moved his head uneasily; then he looked about suddenly and spotted the burly American so close behind him. He roared a brutal curse in some crude foreign tongue and grabbed up the submachine gun and fired—all in the instant. But Chuck, with a superb dive of finely tuned athlete's muscles, had plunged through the door an instant before the bullets tore into the spot where he had been.

Johann was right behind the screaming slugs, running forward with his gun ready and still mouthing curses, when Chuck hit the controls. A spin of two dials, and he slammed home the actuator switch just as Johann burst in on top of him.

Something happened. Something impossible to describe, a twitching sensation perhaps that each of them felt through their entire body, through the entire fabric of space. It was as though their insides were nothing but an immense string on a bass viol and *something* had plucked that string. It was indeed an unusual sensation, and even as it occurred, other things were happening.

The great jet engines gasped and died.

Johann gave Chuck a quick chop with the butt of the gun that plunged him into unconsciousness, then spun about. The stars beyond the window seemed sharper, more clear—and something else.

Light flooded the cabin as the great airship tilted and an immense planet swam into view below. Filling half of the sky, glowing with reflected sunlight. A planet far greater than Earth.

And girded with great glinting rings that floated in space around it.

4

A VICTORIOUS BATTLE
ENDS IN TERROR

The Russian spy was petrified by the sight, stock still and gaping. It was a sight to paralyze anyone, and concealed in the ship behind him Sally had been seized by the same paralysis. But not Jerry! He had been expecting something and had planned for this moment, in fact was scarcely aware of what was happening outside the plane. The instant that Johann had appeared and turned his back Jerry raced soundlessly to the attack, hurling himself forward like a human bullet. In fact, if there had been observers, they would have discovered that he had broken the Olympic record for the ten yard dash. The paralysis was only momentary, and the spy was turning and raising his gun but—too late!—for Jerry was upon him, his arm drawn back, his fist cocked. Before the gun could come up, the decadent enemy jaw felt the full impact of a good American fist in all its fury, and that was the end of the ball game.

Unconscious, the spy stretched his length upon the deck while Sally retrieved the fallen gun and Jerry rubbed his sore hand, which was already beginning to swell and turn red; it felt as if half the bones were broken. At this moment there was a groan from the cubby, and Chuck appeared, rubbing at his sore neck.

"Sorry about that," he said, nodding at the great planet swimming in space beyond the window. "I was kind of rushed. It looks like I misread the decimal on the knob and gave the machine a tenth of a volt instead of a thousandth."

"A *tenth* of a volt did *that!*" Sally gasped, speaking for all of them. "What would have happened if you had used *one hundred and eleven* volts?"

There was awe in Chuck's voice that finally broke the silence that enwrapped them. "A tenth of a volt to go from Earth to Saturn. We have the universe in our palms."

"Isn't the air getting a little thin in here?" Sally asked, suddenly frightened.

"Yes," Jerry responded. "We are in interstellar space where there is no oxygen; that is why the jets stopped. This plane is reasonably airtight, but I imagine our air is leaking out slowly through the compressors. . . ."

"We're going to die!" Sally screamed and began to tear at her hair.

"There, there," Chuck said reassuredly. "We'll work something out." He calmed her and wiped away the sudden beading of sweat that had sprung to her forehead and opened her tight clamped fingers and removed the great handfuls of lovely blond hair.

"We have a problem here," Jerry said, bemusedly.

"But not one that can't be solved!" Chuck smiled, and his friend smiled in return. They would buckle down and lick this thing.

"First off let's tie up our spy friend so he doesn't cause any more trouble," Jerry suggested. "My arm's a bit sore, so you had better take care of that, Chuck. Take plenty of wire and tie him down to one of the chairs in the cabin. And bring back some of those little bottles of vodka. I think Sally will feel better if we pour a couple of those into her. And I'll put my thinking cap on and find a way out of this."

The air in the cabin was a good deal thinner and cooler by the time Chuck came back. The third miniature bottle of vodka rattled against the wall, and Sally was getting a glazed look about the eyes. Jerry pointed at a glowing sphere that had appeared below the twisting plane, while Saturn rode high above them.

"If I'm not mistaken that is Titan, Saturn's biggest moon. I have been watching and we seem to be in her gravitational field and dropping down toward her."

"Lesh go home," Sally said suddenly. "Press the button on your new erector set and lesh go home."

"It's not that easy, Sally darling," Jerry explained,

27

pressing her hand in his in a reassuring manner. "If we activate the cheddite projector now, there is no way of telling where we will end up. Before we throw the switch again, we have to align the resonant frequencies, determine the angle of the solar ecliptic, vibrate the oscillator and. . . ."

"Bullsh-shit," Sally muttered. "Press the frigging button and get us the hell out of here."

"There, there," Chuck said tenderly and led her back to the cabin to curl up in the seat across the aisle from the glowering spy, who had regained consciousness and who was now straining against his unyielding bindings and muttering curses in foreign tongues continuously.

"Here's a thought," Jerry suggested when Chuck had rejoined him at the controls. "We know that Titan has an atmosphere and we seem to be dropping that way. Break out the emergency oxygen cylinders, and we'll hold out until we hit the atmosphere. If there is enough oxygen in the atmosphere, we can do a power landing; if not, a dead stick will have to do. Once down we can calibrate and align the cheddite projector on the solid lunar base so when we activate the mechanism again we will certainly end up back on Earth."

"Great," Chuck enthused. "I'll get the oxy going back there—wait, there it goes by itself." As the pressure dropped, the emergency system had been activated and oxygen masks had dropped down in front of all four hundred seats in the great plane. Jerry put on his mask while Chuck dug out a walkaround cylinder and mask and went back to the cabin. Johann tried to bite him when he offered him the mask but relented as his eyeballs began to bulge and then permitted his enemy to fix the mask in place. Sally was asleep, snoring and gasping alternately, and settled down nicely with the mask and a blanket pulled up over her. After that Chuck went through the plane and tied knots in all the dangling plastic oxygen tubes over all the seats to prevent further loss of this precious gas. By the time he had rejoined Jerry he saw that the moon Titan was swelling quickly below them.

"All okay," Chuck said, dropping into the copilot's seat

28

and pulling at his sore fingers. "How does it look ahead?"

"Not bad. A little lift from the controls, so I think we are at the edge of the atmosphere."

"Doesn't look too darn hospitable," Chuck mused, looking down at the landscape of ice-covered mountains, glaciers, snowfields and barren wastes.

"I don't know." Jerry smiled. "Sort of reminds me of home. So here we go!"

"If that reminds you of home, I'm beginning to see why you came south. Do you realize that the temperature down there is minus two hundred degrees?"

"Doesn't sound too bad," Jerry muttered, all his attention on flying the plane. "Plenty of lift now, but the motors won't catch."

"Probably because the atmosphere consists of methane, ammonia vapor, nitrogen and inert gases—and no oxygen."

"You took the words right out of my mouth. So dead stick it is. Full flaps, drop the landing gear, and let's have the lights."

Down and down they swooped, hurtling toward the jagged frozen peaks below, a nightmare wilderness of fanged rocks and glaring frozen gas that sparkled in multiple colors as the strong lights penetrated the shadows.

"If I can clear that ridge," Jerry murmured, "it may be better on the other side."

Fighting the controls with every particle of his strength and skill, he rode the giant 747 like a behemoth charger of the skies, firm in the saddle and strong on the reins. The great ship quivered as the nose came up, about to stall, while the black fangs of rock reached out hungrily for them. Easing the nose down ever so lightly to prevent the stall, they slid over the escarpment with only feet to spare between the ship and certain death.

"That ice field, there, off to port!" Chuck shouted jubilantly.

"That's the ball game!" Jerry chortled, and tilted the plane into a sharp turn.

Smoothly and easily they drifted down from out of the midnight sky and sped in silence over the smooth ice before dropping to a perfect eighteen-point landing. The air brakes popped up, and the wheel brakes took hold, and instants later they quivered to a halt. The first men on Titan!

"We're the first men on Titan," Chuck said, "and I think maybe we're going to have to stay here."

"Don't be a wet blanket! All we have to do is align the cheddite projector like I said, and wham-o, we're back on Earth."

"That's right. But we were excited and we sort of forgot that the projector is unreliable in an atmosphere."

"So what's the problem? We take off again and fire away from up on top."

"Take off?"

"Sure. Rig a feedline from the oxygen tanks to the engines and away we go."

"Hmmm, yes, that should work. But we have another problem."

"Like what?"

"I've been looking out the window, and that is the third creature with tentacles, a hideous beak, and four bulging eyes that I have seen climb up on the wing."

"Say!" Jerry spun about to see for himself. "Do you think there is life on this moon?"

Before he could answer, a shrill scream pierced through the air, and on the instant both men were running at breakneck speed back to the cabin. Sally was standing on the back of her seat and pointing with quivering finger at the window, still screaming. They followed her finger and smiled and helped her down, still screaming, and tried to soothe her.

"There, there," Jerry said, soothingly, "it's just a native of this moon. All the natives have tentacles, hideous beaks, and four bulging eyes." She screamed louder.

"It can't get in, so don't worry." Chuck laughed, and she stopped screaming. Not because of his reassurance, but because her mask had come off while she screamed, and she was unconscious from deficient oxygenation of her blood. They put her gently back in her seat and adjusted the oxygen flow. The cabin was silent except for the scratch, scratch of the Titanians' beaks on the windows.

"Loosen my bonds," Johann said. "They are too tight and are cutting off my circulation."

"You would try to escape then," Chuck said curtly. "So you will have to suffer just what a Red Commie spy deserves."

"Schweinhund!"

"I have a graduate degree in German so I know what you are saying, and it doesn't bother me."

Sally had recovered consciousness and had listened to this exchange and could not bear it.

"Stop it!" she cried. "Here we are, millions of miles from home, four lost Americans, and you carry on like that. Enough!"

"Silence, woman," Johann said sternly. "I am citizen of Democratic Republic of East Germany and a Soviet agent. *Not* American."

"But you *are*," she insisted. "I know one half of you is East German. But the other half is *American!* Your father was a good American, and that makes you as good an American as any of us."

Silence filled the great cabin, and they saw a large tear form at the corner of each of the spy's eyes and then course down his cheeks. When he spoke, his voice was hoarse with emotion.

"Of course. They lied to me. Made me their own. Never told me I was an American. Deprived me of my birthright. When all the time I was as American as apple pie!"

"Right!" Chuck said, tearing the binding wires free from John's body. "You're one of us."

"I can get a passport, pay income tax, vote in the Presidential election, go to baseball games and eat hot dogs!"

"Darn right!" Jerry shouted as he pumped John's hand. Then Chuck shook his hand, and John turned to kiss Sally but realized maybe he was an American but not *that* American, so he shook her hand as well.

"It's great to be part of the team again." John grinned and knuckled the tears from his cheeks. "What can I do to help?"

31

"We have a little problem," Jerry explained. "We have to take off so the cheddite projector will be able to work, but there is no oxygen in the atmosphere here. So we have to rig a supply of oxygen from the tanks here to the engines. . . ."

"I'm afraid that's out," Chuck said after mumbling some quick equations to himself. "I've worked out the amount of oxygen the engines need and how much we have in the tanks and I figure we have just enough to move us one hundred and ten feet. Allowing no time for engine warm-up."

"Then that's out." Chuck grimaced, striking his fist into his open palm. "So we'll just have to find another way."

"That seems sort of obvious." John smiled. "Being an American has really stirred up my old brain box, and I'm thinking in a realistic capitalistic way, instead of slavishly socialistic, and believe me, it works wonders! The answer is right outside that window."

They all looked and Sally started screaming again at the sight of the beaks, eyes and tentacles. John went on.

"While I was sitting there, I had plenty of time to look at those critturs and think about them. What attracted them to this plane? Not just curiosity, they don't seem that type, but *something*. Not heat, our temperature would be like a blowtorch to them. And I noticed that they are most thick out there around the air compressors."

"Oxygen!" Jerry said, snapping his fingers. "Of course. As it leaks out, they suck it up. They like oxygen. Which proves that this planet once had an Earthlike atmosphere, and these creatures are nothing but degenerate descendants of the former inhabitants. They must have a source of oxygen. All we have to do is find it and we can take off. We're going out there."

"The Titanians will attack us for the oxygen in our blood," Chuck said, realistically.

"Then we'll fight," John said, jaw set firmly. "And they'll know they've been in a fracas."

Preparations were quickly made. They sawed through the floor to gain access to the forward cargo hold, where the team's luggage was stored. Since the temperature outside was 200 degrees below zero, they had to bundle up warmly. Each of them put on layer after layer of football clothes and pads and helmets to protect their heads, slinging portable oxygen tanks at their waists. Sally was busy too, using needle and thread that she found in her purse to make them all gloves from the cheerleaders' uniforms. Chuck wore his own uniform with his big number one blazoned front and back. They found number two for Jerry, who, though he could play football of course, did not go out for it since he was too busy captaining the hockey team, as well as captaining the fencing and chess teams. Since John was new to the team and not enrolled in the school, he smilingly settled for ninety-nine.

"We need weapons," Chuck said, taking command of the team. "I'll use the ax from the rescue kit."

"Heat is their enemy, so the oxyhydrogen torch is mine," Jerry added.

"If I use the alcohol from the first-aid kit, I can clean all the lubrication from my submachine gun, and it will fire at two hundred degrees below zero," John concluded.

"Here we go, team," Chuck said. "Lock the door behind us, Sally, and only open it if we knock three times."

"Good luck, boys," Sally said, and patted each rugged shoulder as it rushed by her into the fight.

The battle was joined. Evidently the smell of hot oxygen drove the Titanians into a frenzy of lust, and they hurled themselves to the attack with a terrible fury. Back to back the Americans faced them and coolly wreaked havoc in their hideous ranks. Tirelessly the great arm of Chuck rose and fell like a butcher's over the block, and tentacles and eye-bulging heads flew in all directions, green ichor spurting like rain. Nor was Jerry being sluggard. His torch cut through the advancing ranks of the enemy like a sword of victory, sizzling them into dismembered and cooked fragments. Coolly, John sighted his gun and fired only single shots, yet every single shot went true, right between the second and third eye of a hideous head and into the malformed brain behind it. And still they came. And still they died. To face the enemy the comrades had to climb the mounting pile of dead bodies that grew about

33

them, and so the slaughter went on until the last of the vile attackers met his well-deserved fate. Smoke curled from the hot barrel of the gun, ichor dripped from the now-lowered ax, and the oxyhydrogen torch was turned off to save the gas.

"Well done, men," Chuck said, and they clambered and slipped down the forty-foot-high mountain of corpses to the ground. "Anyone hurt?"

"A few scratches." The others laughed. "Nothing that counts."

"Then let's go get that oxygen. During the battle I noticed that most of the Titanians were coming from that direction, and if you look closely at that ridge, you will see a kind of white band toward the bottom. I'll bet my bottom dollar that that is frozen oxygen!"

They hurried toward the ridge, but before they could reach it, tragedy struck.

A shrill scream pierced the thin Titanian atmosphere, and they stopped as one and spun about on their heels. To see a sight so awful that it would be branded in their memories forever.

The cabin door stood open, and dropping down from the wing were a dozen of the hideous Titanians.

And carried in their midst, wrapped about by slimy tentacles, was the screaming, struggling, lovely form of Sally Goodfellow.

5

DEFEAT RUDELY SNATCHED
FROM THE JAWS OF VICTORY

Paralysis gripped them, but only momentarily. Before the enemy had slithered another foot with the captive girl, the vengeful Americans were hot on their trail, weapons awave.

"Chin up, Sally!" Chuck bellowed. "Here we come!"

"I don't think . . . she can hear you," Jerry answered between gasping breaths. "She has no oxygen tank, so she is already unconscious."

And so she was, her screams were silenced, and she hung limply down the repulsive back of her captor. The fleeing Titanians looked back, easy enough to do since it could be seen now that they had four more eyes in the backs of their heads, and upon spotting the rushing avengers, they took defensive action. Half their number stopped and waited, frigid grasping tentacles raised for the attack. The battle was quickly joined. Heads flew right and left, and sundered tentacles littered the ground like so many salamis, and the Earthmen barely slowed in their rush. But more were waiting for them, and they were dispatched just as neatly. Now the coast was clear, the last of the rear guard dead, and only the fleeing Titanian with the unconscious girl across its shoulders remained.

But the holding action had succeeded in gaining this disgusting creature needed time, and just as they were onto the thing, it darted down a gaping trench in the ground. Without a thought, other than to save Sally, the three companions instantly followed it into the unknown. This was raw courage, the spirit that built the frontier and put men on the Moon. Unhesitatingly they went to whatever fate faced them ahead.

As it twisted, the trench deepened and then plunged

into a black cave mouth. This cave was dimly illuminated by some sort of natural growth on the walls, apparently a plant or vegetable of some kind that gave off a ghastly greenish glow just as do some forms of plankton in the seas of Earth. There was just enough light to make out the fleeing figure of the kidnapper, and they went after it at full speed. It darted into a side tunnel before they could catch up with it, and then into another, always just outside their reach as though toying with them, leading them on. Give them credit, they did not consider their own peril for an instant but instead plunged on. They were just upon the fleeing Titanian when it emerged into a larger cave and scuttled slitheringly across its rough floor. After it they went, and they were just about to seize and render it when a burst of illumination flooded down upon them. By reflex they shielded their eyes, and when they could look up, they saw the source of this unexpected light.

From floor to rough ceiling high above the great chamber in the rock was covered with the light-emitting plants. Ledges ran about the walls, and on the ledges stood numberless Titanians with whips, and upon a given signal they had begun to whip the simple vegetable life. Apparently this abuse stirred the hapless plants to unusual activity, and they burned with cold light, rippling in agony beneath the merciless assault. But the Titanians had no pity, even if they had had the capacity for pity, and lashed on. With their eyes now accustomed to the light the Earthmen saw a sight that made their blood run cold.

Against the far wall, on a dais or throne of crudely carved stone, sat a Titanian at least twice as big as all the others, twice as ugly too, outdoing them in loathsomeness. A rough crown of some shining metal sat on its head, and there was a tremendous but crudely cut diamond set into the front of it. But these facts they were scarcely aware of, for what froze their gaze and raised their hearts into the throats was the sight of Sally held in the thing's tentacles while other of its tentacles caressed her ivory limbs revealed through the rents in her thin summer frock that was partially torn away from her fair body. Yet, under this repulsive embrace, Sally was strangely unmoving. In fact her

36

ivory limb was looking a lot more like ivory all the time since, on second glance it could be seen that it was frozen solid.

"She's frozen solid," Jerry gasped.

"She was the best," Chuck gulped and took off his helmet and held it before his chest.

"Don't give up hope yet," John whispered. "If we can get her out of this, we can. . . ."

"Eef you attempt too reesist, you vill all *die!*" the creature on the throne hissed, laying off caressing his prisoner long enough to signal with a tentacle. Instantly all of the entrances to the cave were filled with Titanians carrying long, curved daggers, shaped very much like Arab scimitars except for a lack of a guard of any kind. Bubbling laughter came from the king as he saw their looks of astonishment.

"You are surprised, no? Beefore thees you faced only my oxygen workers driven mad by your hot oxygen. Now you see my finest troops."

"But—you speak our language?" Jerry said.

"Naturally. We have crystal detector radios of immense power, and we listen to your radio broadcasts and have learned your tongue. Always we wait for the rockets to land, the first explorers to arrive. Our plans are made. We kill, capture the ship and leave this barren world, where we are trapped with an ever-diminishing supply of oxygen. At last we have done this! You will be held prisoner and tortured to tell us everything you know about how to operate your flying ship and then you will die horribly. Seize them!"

At this command the minions surged forward and the light plants writhed under increased whipping. But their prey was not that easy to capture! With a single voice the Earthmen shouted *Geronimo!* and attacked the king in unison. It seized four immense blades from behind its throne, but before it could wield them, a single well-placed bullet found its target between its third and fourth eye, and it slumped in death, and Sally slid from its now-loosened embrace.

37

"Grab Sally before she hits the ground!" Jerry shouted. "She might break!"

This was a real danger, frozen solid as she was, and the two men forgot everything to save the woman they loved and leaped and caught her and raised her gently in their arms while John stood behind them, his gun on full automatic, spraying screaming death to the howling hordes. Yet still they came on, daggers raised for vengeance, and John flashed a brief look over his shoulder to see that Sally was safe. As soon as he saw this, he raised his gun and in a burst of bullets shot the whippers from their balconies. Their agonized cries ended in splats upon the floor, and with the whipping stopped, the cavern was once again plunged into stygian gloom.

"Ich mochte ein Einzelzimmer mit Bad im ersten Stock!" *

Jerry shouted this gutturally in German, knowing that the other two would understand this language, also knowing that the Titanians spoke English and would understand anything spoken in this language. And it worked! He threw Sally, frozen possibly for eternity in a position of stark fear, over one shoulder and felt Chuck seize her ankles and knew, despite the darkness, that John had his hand on Chuck's shoulder. Soundlessly he led them to the door and pushed it open, stepping into the black unknown beyond, fearlessly, preferring that to the certain death awaiting them in the throne room, from which there now emerged a great clashing and screaming.

"Well done," John whispered. "They're killing each other back there, thinking that we are still in their midst. I've closed the door and sealed it—so let's have some light."

Jerry lit the welding torch, and they saw that they were in a roughly hewn tunnel that vanished into the darkness ahead.

"I'll take Sally now," Chuck said, his deed as good as

* "I spotted a door behind the throne, so grab onto me and we can escape that way."

38

word, relieving Jerry of his precious frozen burden. "Lead on and make *tracks* because my oxygen is almost gone."

And tracks they did make at a steady ground-eating jog of over seven mph, the only sound the thud of their feet and their hoarse breathing eating away at the diminishing oxygen supply. Suddenly, far ahead, they saw a light patch of darkness in which swam distant points of light.

"The end of the tunnel," Jerry said, switching off the torch. "And those look like stars or I'll eat my hat. Be alert because we have no idea what, or what *thing*, may be waiting out there."

Silently and grimly they advanced, weapons ready, to burst suddenly out upon the icy plain. They were alone, close beside a cliff and not too distant from the 747, which rested solidly, windows glowing a warm welcome.

"Look," Jerry pointed, drawing their attention to a white band of material in the cliff and to the chunks of the same white substance on the ground. "I'll be darned if that's not *oxygen*—and old kingy had a private tunnel for a constant supply . . ."

"No"—gasp—"oxygen!" John gasped, and they hurried quickly to the plane.

With new tanks snapped into place and a fresh supply of the life-giving substance filling their lungs, they were ready for anything, and it was Jerry who spoke, detailing a carefully worked-out plan.

"All the Titanians out there are dead—but I'll bet dollars to doughnuts that there will be plenty of live ones along mighty soon. So we had better get ready and get out of here before they put a crimp in our plans—after all, we can't kill all of them."

"Wish we could," John growled, and the others growled instant agreement before Jerry went on.

"So here is what we do. We dig out the frozen oxygen and fill the forward hold with it, that's the job for you two. While you're doing that, I'll hook up feedpipes from this hold to all the engines and also rig an electric heater in the hold. When the hold is full, we seal it, turn on the heater, the solid oxygen sublimates to a gas, is piped to the engines, we turn on the fuel flow—"

"—and away we go!" Chuck enthused. "Foolproof. But what about Sally?"

At his words their happy expressions faded, and they looked at the hapless girl, still frozen in an attitude of horror, who was leaning against the corner of the wall by the bar. It was John who cracked that frozen moment of gloom, clappng his chums upon the shoulder.

"Don't worry, I told you she would be all right, but no time to explain now. Let's put her in one of the johns with a hunk of frozen oxygen, and she'll keep OK."

They went to work with a will. Working like maniacs, they dug and tore at the seam of oxygen, dragging the frozen chunks back on a sled improvised from a stretcher used by the football team. Nor was Jerry just sitting on his duff, for with the energy and skill of a mechanical genius, which he was, he had replumbed fuel lines and air ducts, rigged an electric heater from torn-out galley stoves and generally fixed the great engines to operate in an oxygen-free atmosphere. The hold was almost full, and they were trundling up the last load of oxygen when a shrill and alien wailing could be heard across the frozen plain.

"Here they come," John said grimly. "Load the oxy aboard and I'll hold them off until we're ready to go."

And this stalwart American, so long misled but now returned to his homeland, was as good as his word. He ran forward shouting a battle cry, whether it was "Remember Pearl Harbor!" or "Remember the *Maine!*" or whatever is not important; what *is* important is that one man faced that ravening alien horde with a smile upon his lips. Shot after well-placed shot rang out, each one bringing down at least three of the screeching, dagger-waving Titanians, and the attack was slowed. But their numbers pressed on, and by sheer weight they forced him back, step by reluctant step, until he was almost under the wing of the *Pleasantville Eagle.*

"This is my last clip," he shouted back over his shoulder, pulling the trigger on the instant and exploding to green shreds the head of an importune enemy.

"There!" a welcome voice called out in reply, and three

40

dark cylinders flew over his head. "Put a bullet through each of those and get inside. We're ready to go!"

And he had just *three* bullets left. Only a superb marksman could have hit those small targets under the tricky light of Saturn, exhausted and faced by an attacking horde of monsters. But he did it, almost casually, a smile playing about his lips all the time. Three shots rang out, almost as one, and each container burst into coruscating flame. Wails of pain and anger broke out from the Titanians, who were forced back by the only thing they really feared. *Heat!* Taking advantage of the moment's respite, John dived for the doorway and slammed it shut behind him.

"Oxygen pressure up to two atmospheres and still rising," Chuck called out, bent over a pressure gauge that had been rigged in the floor leading to the hold below.

"Then hold onto your hats because here we go!" Jerry called out jubilantly from the pilot's seat as he jammed the throttle home and fired up the outboard starboard engine.

They held their breaths, unknowingly, as the engine whined over slowly, protesting at these strange conditions. Over and over it turned while the Titanians pressed close for the attack, whining and grumbling and not catching at all, slower and slower.

"The batteries are almost dead," Jerry cried. "Turn out all the lights, everything that draws electricity, even the monomatic toilets, so I can try again."

Darkness fell instantly inside the plane as the switches were thrown, and they waited in hushed silence as Jerry threw the starting switch again.

"What were those bombs?" John asked. "I didn't know we had any explosive aboard."

"Just something I rigged out of used oxygen cylinders in case you needed some help. Filled with jet fuel and chunks of frozen oxygen. The fuel melted the oxygen, which pressurized the cylinders, which blew up when you shot them, and the inflammable mixture was ignited by your hot bullets."

His words were interrupted by a sudden popping explosion from the engine, and they held their breaths while a

41

cloud of smoke and flame was ejected from the exhaust. The popping slowed, almost stopped, picked up again; then the engine burst into the full-throated roar of full power, drowning out forever the screams of the inciner- ated Titanians who were blown away by the exhaust. His two companions pounded the pilot on the back as the other engines caught one after another until the great ship was vibrating with barely restrained power. Chuck slid into the copilot's seat and readied himself at the controls.

"I just had a thought," he said as he reached to release the wheel brakes. "Did you align the cheddite projector?"

"I thought you would never ask." Jerry laughed. "It was the first thing I did while the oxygen was warming up. She's now lined up to fourteen decimal points and A-OK and ready to go. And I've done all the settings and locked the controls. All we have to do is take this barge up to thirty thousand feet, aim the nose directly at Polaris, also called the North Star, point the starboard wing at the out- ermost point of Saturn's ring—and press the firing button! We'll appear at twenty-eight thousand nine hundred and fifty feet over central Kansas, give or take a few feet."

"Great! So here we go!"

The *Pleasantville Eagle* turned ponderously about and started back down the ice in the very tracks it had made on landing, crushing and incinerating the surviving Titan- ians as it went. Faster and faster until it was yearning to leap from the ground. Then, throttles full back, it hurled itself into the air, free of the jagged crags below, and pointed its nose towards mighty Saturn.

"What a moment!" Chuck enthused.

"Yes," Jerry said, and the smile was suddenly erased from his face. "Everything is fine—except for poor Sally."

At these words Chuck's smile went the way of the other's, and only John still smiled across the cabin.

"I told you not to worry," he said, and instantly four worried eyes, two burning black, two icy blue, were fixed upon him.

"What do you mean?" Jerry choked out for them both.

"Here is what we are going to do."

42

6

LOATHSOME GARNISHEE AND
A MINDLESS HUSK

"Before I realized I was an American, you will remember that I was a secret Soviet agent. Some strange things happened then, let me tell you, but that is another story altogether. But I did a lot of training in Siberia, and on one secret mission there I took an advanced degree in brain surgery, which had to do with something else, but while I was working at the underground hospital in Novaya Zemlya, I got to chatting with the other doctors, you know, sort of talking shop, and they showed me some things they were working on. One thing I remember was deep freezing, always a kind of problem in Siberia, as you can imagine, and they had worked out a secret technique for reviving people who were caught out in blizzards and things and were frozen solid just like Sally back there in the john."

"And you know . . . ?" Jerry choked over the words.

"Sure, I took it all in and could do it standing on my head. All we need is the services of a well-equipped hospital with hypothermia equipment and a few odds and ends. Just turn me loose, and in a couple of hours you'll have your Sally again just as good as new."

"Yippee!" Jerry shouted and pulled the plane up in an immense curve toward Saturn. "Pleasantville General Hospital and Rest Home here we come!"

Upward they climbed and on course, and the altimeter needle slowly unwound. Chuck was at the controls of the cheddite projector and testing the circuits when he called out, "Jerry—we're getting unwanted resonance in the beta kappa circuit."

"Must be instability in the woofer. I'll take care of it." He waved John toward the pilot's seat. "Take over and

43

keep her on course. Align the nose with Polaris, the wing-tip with Saturn's rings and sing out when the needle on the sensitive radar altimeter touches thirty thousand feet."

"Roger," John said firmly and took the controls.

Higher and higher the great wings of the *Pleasantville Eagle* soared with John resolutely at the controls, Jerry and Chuck laboring over the vital circuitry of the cheddite projector.

"Coming up on point zero," John called back. "How are you doing there?"

"In the green—ready whenever you are."

"Okay, watch it now. Ship aligned perfectly, altimeter unwinding. Ready . . . five . . . four . . . three . . . two . . . one . . . HACK!"

And a firm thumb was thrust home on the activator button.

Once again that *strange* sensation plucked at the very fiber of their beings as the kappa radiation hurled them headlong into the lambda dimension to emerge once again in normal space. And the engines stopped.

"I think we're a *leetle* high," Jerry laughed, looked at the green globe of the planet far below them. "But gravity will bring us down quick enough."

Chuck was squinting out of the window, a quizzical expression pulling at his features. "Funny," he muttered, "but I don't see the Moon."

"Not only that," John answered, a look of concentration marked on his face, "but the constellations just aren't *right*."

They nodded silent agreement, and when Jerry spoke, he spoke for them all.

"I hate to say it, guys, but I'm afraid that isn't Earth down there. Not only that, but I'm afraid it isn't even any planet in our solar system. Perhaps something has gone wrong with the cheddite projector. I'll check it out."

"No," John said huskily. He was staring at the sensitive radar altimeter like a bird petrified by a snake, sweat suddenly bursting out on his brow. "I'm afraid I goofed. All those years behind the iron curtain didn't really do me any good. Jerry, you told me to sound off when the altimeter hit thirty thousand feet, right?"

"Bang on."

"Well, and I hate to say this gang, all the planes I have ever flown have always had altimeters that read in meters, so I converted feet to meters and let you know when we hit that spot."

"Approximately one-third of our needed altitude," Jerry intoned in a hollow voice. "Still inside the deep atmosphere which interferes with the kappa radiation."

John was no longer smiling as he uneasily eyed the great, cocked fist of Chuck that was slowly being drawn back into firing position. Jerry came between them and calmed them down.

"Easy does it. Anyone can make a mistake—and we've gotten out of worse pinches before. Remember that old king of the Titanians and what happened to him!"

They all laughed at that memory, and the tension was eased. John lowered his head, chagrined.

"Gee, I'm sorry. Something must have snapped inside my head for me to goof up like that. We'll get out of this. Land on that planet, align the cheddite projector, then take off, and home we go!"

"And we can put some more ice in the head with Sally. She'll keep OK."

After that it was just waiting as they fell. The cabin heaters were on, and fresh Titanian oxygen was being pumped into the air, and soon they could peel off the extra layers of clothing. Chuck found some cans of cola, and they thawed and drank them, pretending not to notice when John poured seven miniatures of bourbon into his. They knew he felt bad about the mistake, and they were good enough sports not to rub it in. More frozen oxygen was packed in with Sally, still exhibiting a look of frozen horror, and they took turns grabbing a little shut-eye, not knowing what would befall them on the planet ever growing larger below. When the first wisps of atmosphere began to whistle against the skin of the ship, Chuck took the controls and waggled them.

"Almost there. Better strap in because this might be a bit rough. I think we picked up some velocity in the fall."

They certainly had. Air tore at the wings until the edges began to glow and the deicer boots burned away. Chuck stayed rock-firm at the wheel and sent them bouncing in a great arc out into space again only to fall back once more into the atmosphere. Again and again he did this until their great speed was slowed to under a thousand miles per hour, and only then did he let the ship sink deeper into the atmosphere.

"Oceans, continents," Jerry said. "Almost like Earth. Makes you kind of homesick."

"That big continent, the one there," John said, pointing. "I think that one looks the *most* like North America."

"Sure enough," Chuck agreed. "And that's the way we are going to head."

Heavy cloud layers covered the continent in question as they swooped in low over what could have been one on Earth—how far away now! A great storm center seemed to be active here and Jerry pulled up to go over the top of it. Apparently thunderstorms were worse on this planet than on Earth, for lightning glared and exploded continually within the clouds and the rumble of thunder could be heard even through the insulated cabin walls. They went on seeking clear weather on the far side of the immense storm.

"Good news, guys," Jerry chortled. "I've turned off the oxygen flow since this atmosphere seems to have more than enough to run the engines on."

"You know," Chuck mused, "there is something kind of funny about that thunder and lightning. If the idea wasn't so downright dim and stupid I would almost say that—"

The great 747 bucked suddenly, and there was a solid thud felt through the metal fabric and a hole more than a yard in diameter appeared in the port wing.

"—those were explosions out there, shells and bombs and stuff, as though a war were going on."

While he mused over this, Jerry had pulled back on the wheel and fed full power to the engines and the leviathan of the skies roared up and away from the tumult below.

"I don't think we should mix in a war," John opined.

Jerry nodded agreement. "Particularly since that hole in the wing ruptured our main fuel tank and we only have about fifteen minutes' fuel left."

"That is annoying," Chuck agreed. "Better buckle your seat belts, guys," and he turned on the *seat belts* and *no smoking* signs as he said this.

The *Pleasantville Eagle* clawed its way back into the sky reaching for altitude to stretch its meager fuel supply to the upmost, fighting to clear the immense area of the strange battlefield below. They were above the clouds, droning away merrily, while the fuel needles loudly clicked, one by one, against their bottom pins. Then came the moment they had awaited and feared as, one by one, the greedy engines sucked in the last drops of fuel, then gurgled and gasped into silence. The instant the powerful thrust stopped the ship fell off into a dive, plunged toward the woolly clouds below it, diving into their misty embrace. None of the three comrades said anything, but if pulses hammered faster and jaws were clenched more firmly, who was to blame them? *Anything* could be waiting below the clouds.

What was waiting, they saw when they plunged through the bottom of the fleecy layer, was not very much of anything at all. From horizon to horizon, shadowed by the thick clouds above, lay a sandy waste barren of life of any kind.

"I don't think we should land down there," John said, speaking for all of them.

Jerry stretched the glide with all his considerable talent, but though he could fight, he could not win against the inexorable grip of gravity that clutched at the 747 with greedy fingers. The featureless desert flashed by below them, ever closer, and dimly far ahead a range of mountains appeared.

"Quick, the glasses!" Chuck exclaimed, leaning forward and peering intently into the distance. John slapped them into his hand, and in an instant he had them trained on the ground. "There's a fort there of some kind, I can see a flag waving over it, and explosions all around it, more fighting

I guess. Yes, there are vehicles of some kind circling it, firing, and guns on the wall firing back. I can see the defenders now! Why, they're almost human except maybe they have an extra couple of arms, but what does that matter!"

"Who are they fighting?" Jerry asked, concentrating firmly on the controls.

"Hard to tell—wait—one of their cars just got blown over, the driver is crawling out and . . . ugggh!"

"Ugggh?"

"That's the word for it. A thing with a sort of repulsive purplish yellow body like a tree trunk with sort of openings all over it, four legs like smaller tree trunks and black tentacles sprouting on top where a real person would have a head."

"Well that's enough for me!" Jerry shouted for them all. "We just have to come in on the side of the humanoids and show those uggghs what real humans can do."

"Right!" Chuck agreed. "But what *can* we do?"

"You've got a point there. Any ideas, guys?"

It was John, trained spy and saboteur, who quickly came up with the answer. "All the seats dismount easily. Make a turn and come back over the enemy and we'll show them what *men* can do against those purple scum."

And show them they did. As the *Pleasantville Eagle* swooped down like its avenging namesake, from the opened emergency doors on each side dropped a stream of metal seats. Dropped straight and true as though aimed by computing bombsights, each seat plunging headlong onto one of the fleeing vehicles.

And the ruse worked. It was not obvious how much damage the chairborne attack had done, but it had apparently broken the spirit of the enemy, for they now fled with their tentacles tucked between their legs, across the desert to vanish in the range of hills. Cheers broke out in the cabin, and through the whistling slipstream, echoing cheers could be heard from the defenders below. Jerry whipped the plane about in a tight turn and with their last bit of speed brought the *Eagle* safely home to roost on the smooth desert floor, braking to a stop in the shadow of the fort's high walls.

"Here," Jerry said, passing on the electric razor to the others after he had used it. "Let's neaten up, give these guys the right impression."

They all agreed on this, and by the time they had used deodorant too and brushed the last green stain of Titanian ichor from their clothing, combed their hair and renewed Sally's frozen oxygen a reception committee was waiting for them at the foot of the folding stairway that automatically slipped out of the plane's side when the entrance was opened. Step by step they descended to the historical moment when humanoid met humanoid for the first time across the trackless oceans of space. Each group examined the other with unabashed curiosity. What the aliens saw was, of course, the three Americans. What the Americans saw were three aliens. They had very smooth, white, shining skin, and when the first one raised his steel helmet in greeting, they saw that the humanoids were hairless as well. The pupils of their eyes were shaped like the number 8 and were bright pink. They wore no clothes but instead were draped about with a leather harness from which were suspended a number of weapons as well as other items not easily identifiable. Then, upon a shouted signal from their leader—the one in front whose helmet was gold instead of black like the others—they pulled out their swords and raised them in salute. The three Americans jumped to attention and returned the salute snappily, although John raised his clenched fist first before remembering and quickly touching his forefinger to his brow, hand and forearm straight, longest way up and shortest way down, like the others. Then the steel of the swords rasped back into the scabbards, and the leader stepped forward.

"Sdrah stvoo ee tyeh," he gurgled in a deep voice.

"Though we are strangers from across the deeps of space and do not speak your fine though incomprehensible language, nevertheless we come in peace and bring you greetings from the men of planet Earth, and particularly the United States," Jerry answered.

49

"Daw braw yeh oo traw," John said. "He was just saying hello in Russian, and I told him good morning back."

"Jumping Jehoshaphat," Chuck whispered. "You don't think they're Commies, do you?" They all stepped backward cautiously.

"No Commies," the leader said, smiling a toothless grin, since he had a bony ridge instead of teeth, and raising his helmet again in greeting. "We are the Ormoloo who battle against the repulsive Garnishee from whom you saved us and for which we will be internally grateful."

"You speak English pretty well for an Ormoloo," Jerry said.

"For many years our powerful radio receivers have been picking up radio transmissions from your planet, and we have studied them and have learned your language. Men of Earth and of the great country the United States of America, I return your greetings and welcome you in peace to our planet Domite. Everything we have is at your disposal on this most momentous occasion. A banquet has been prepared in your honor, and we beg you to grace our table with your noble democratic presences."

"Lead the way," Chuck said, and they did.

The three Earthmen looked around with wonder at the inside of the fort. In some way it was very much like a desert fort on Earth with plastered walls and a crenellated top above the firing step. But here the resemblance ended, for the Ormoloo had a fantastic assortment of strange weapons, some of which defied description. They then and there determined to examine these later to see how they worked. The leader, who had introduced himself as Steigen-Sterben, turned and smiled his toothless grin back at them.

"Later you must examine our weapons and see how they work," he said.

They nodded agreement and entered the banquet hall, where each was conducted to a place of honor at the long table. The table was bare except for a clay bowl before each place filled with cool water. After they were all seated, Steigen-Sterben raised his hand and all of the heads were lowered as he spoke.

"Oh, Great Spirit who lives in the Other World above, we thank you for what you have provided." The prayer over, they raised their heads, and Chuck nudged Jerry in the ribs and whispered.

"They must be great guys, with religion and everything," and Jerry agreed.

Now the waiters appeared carrying great baskets, and with three-pronged tines, they scooped out mounds of what looked like green grass and deposited them on the bare table before each diner. As soon as they had all been served, Steigen-Sterben signaled, and they all fell to with a will, bending over and munching up mouthfuls of the grass. All except the three Earthmen, who were not sure what to do until Jerry broke the ice and picked up some of it and put it in his mouth and chewed and swallowed quickly, then drained his water bowl.

"Jumping horseflies," he whispered, "That grass is grass."

"I see you are not eating," Steigen-Sterben said. "I must apologize for our simple fare, but we Ormoloo are strict vegetarians, for religious principles of course, and never vary our diet."

"Well, some of my best friends are vegetarians," Jerry rushed to explain so no insult would be felt. "But we guys here we're, well, omnivores for the most part. But go ahead and eat, don't let us stop you."

"No insult felt," Steigen-Sterben mumbled through a luscious mouthful. "We'll be through pretty soon."

The three companions looked around at the blank walls and sipped their water, and sure enough, inside of a minute the Ormoloo had finished their banquet, the last blade lapped up and the table licked clean.

"Let me tell you about this war," Steigen-Sterben lowed, licking a last green fragment from his lips. "For over ten thousand of your Earth years we have been locked in this struggle, for the Garnishee are ruthless demons and would kill us all, horribly, if they had their way. So back and forth the war rages, for we are evenly matched, and it appears it will go on for ten thousand years more."

"Would you mind my asking why you are fighting?" Chuck asked.

"No, I wouldn't."

"Why are you fighting?"

"We fight to maintain our free way of life, to worship the Great Spirit in our own manner and to wipe out to the last evil individual of the hideous Garnishee."

"Would you mind my asking why you dislike them?" Jerry said. "I mean other than the fact they are pretty nasty-looking and all that."

"I hesitate to tell you, to profane your ears with the horrors of their way of life."

"We can take it," John said, speaking for them all.

"Rather than tell you, for it is hard to speak the unspeakable, let me show you."

At a signal the lights dimmed, and a hidden movie projector sprang to life, using one white wall as a screen. Strange music sobbed and wailed, and credits and titles in an unknown script appeared. The film was in color and seemed to be well made, except that the voice over was in a totally incomprehensible language. When the credits ended, the three friends gasped because the speaker was a disgusting *Ormoloo,* with all his repulsive details in living color. His black tentacles waved, and it could be seen that one of the openings in the central trunk was a mouth that opened and closed. A ring of eyes ran around what would have been the creature's waist, had it had a waist.

"Ugly beggar," Jerry said, and the others nodded agreement.

"Not only that," Steigen-Sterben said, "but they smell very badly as well."

Now the creature on the screen rose, and picking up a stick, it stumped over on its four postlike legs to a diagram, which it began to point at with the stick. The diagram was a simple drawing of an Ormoloo with dotted lines across many different parts of his body.

"What does it mean?" John asked.

52

"Unhappily"—Steigen-Sterben sighed—"you will find out quickly enough."

They did, indeed, find out quickly enough. The scene changed, and a dead Ormoloo was stretched out on a wooden block while the speaker sawed him apart with a powerful bandsaw.

"Enough!" Jerry shouted, springing to his feet and knocking over his chair. The film vanished, and the lights came back on. Steigen-Sterben sat with head lowered and, finally, explained in a hushed voice.

"This was what I dared not speak of. The Garnishee seek only to capture us and *eat* us, for they are monsters."

"Monsters indeed!" Chuck roared, jumping up and knocking over his chair. "I know I speak for us all when I say that we will give you every aid within our power to wipe these fiends from the face of your fair planet!"

All the Earthmen nodded solemn agreement, and as one, the Ormoloo jumped to their feet and saluted and cheered themselves hoarse, shouting, "Hip, hip, HOORAY!" over and over again.

"And I think I know a way to do that," Jerry said thoughtfully. "I am considering a weapon far stronger than anything you have here, a weapon I could build that would wipe out your enemies to the last fiend."

"You wouldn't," Steigen-Sterben said, smiling broadly and putting a friendly arm or two around Jerry's shoulders, "care to tell me about it, would you, old man?"

"Not just yet. I have to work some bugs out of it before I do that. But first we have something more pressing to worry about. Before the frozen oxygen runs out, we have to do something about Sally."

"Could I examine your hospital?" John asked.

"Of course," Steigen-Sterben said, "but you must not expect it to be up to the fine standards of a hospital like your Pleasantville General Hospital and Rest Home. . . ."

"You've heard about that *here?*" Chuck gasped.

"Of course. I listened to the radio program myself about its unique modern wonders and remember it clearly.

That is why I say ours are crude by comparison. You see we Ormoloo have no pain nerves or bloodstream as you do." To prove the point he drew his sword and plunged it through the body of the Ormoloo next to him who never batted an eyelid but went on licking a grass blade from his hand. When the sword came out, only a tiny hole could be seen that instantly sealed up. "Our blood goes from cell to cell by osmosis so we need neither heart nor blood vessels. Also, our bodies are very resistant to infections. Our hospitals are, well, just a sort of wooden table, a couple of knives and saws and a lot of needles and thread. If parts are too damaged to save, we hack them off, that's about all."

"Yes, I understand," John mused. "But I had something a little more complex in mind for Sally. Look—you must have machine shops and tools, things like that?"

"Of course. There is a complete machine shop here for servicing our weapons and machines."

"Then that's the answer. I can make the instruments I will need; it won't take long. I'll fix things up while you guys get Sally in here."

He was as good as his word, for no sooner had the two others put on their insulated gloves and carried Sally in from the refrigerated john than they found him in the middle of a well-equipped hospital room.

"I'll need some help. Are either of you up to assisting?"

"I have a graduate degree in open-heart surgery," Chuck said. "Will that help?"

"Good. You can pass me the instruments. What about you, Jerry?"

"My only graduate medical degree is in proctology, so maybe I better just watch."

The newly built revasculator pumped, throbbed and gurgled, the hysterisis-annihilator hissed, the corpuscular reconstitutor clicked passionately—and all these machines under the deft control of John, who indeed was a master surgeon. Beneath his tender ministrations Sally's tender body, still clad in the remnants of her gay summer frock, relaxed and lost the glassy frozen look. Within minutes she

54

had softened a good deal, though, of course, her heart was not beating, nor was she breathing.

"The intravascular oxygenator is supplying oxygen directly to her brain cells," John said calmly, while his hands flashed busily about their tasks. "As you know if the blood supply to the brain is cut off for more than two minutes, the brain begins to deteriorate, and even if the patient lives, it will be only as a mindless husk. We can only hope that Sally froze quickly back there on Titan, or she will be a beautiful but mindless husk. Now, stand back if you please, for I shall apply two hundred and thirty volts of direct current with these paddles directly to her heart which will surprise it into beating again, and she will, I hope, be restored to young and vital life."

The paddles were applied, the switch thrown, Sally's body contracted with the shock, and she leaped a yard into the air. When she came down, her eyes were wide open, and she put her knuckles to her mouth and screamed loudly over and over again.

"Husk. . . ." Both the young men who loved her sighed.

"Perhaps not," said John, injecting a note of hope into what appeared to be an inevitable and tragic occasion. "Perhaps she was frozen so fast her memory was frozen as well, and she thinks she is still a prisoner of the loathsome Titanians."

"It's us, Sally," Jerry said hopefully. "You're safe, do you hear that, safe!"

She looked around her, dazedly, her eyes still empty of anything resembling intelligence.

7

A GREAT VICTORY—
BUT TRAGEDY STRIKES

"Well, thanks for trying, John," Jerry said wearily.

"Yeah," Chuck added in the same gloom-ridden tone of voice. "You did your best. But it was just too late. She is a hapless vegetable forever."

"Vegetable, my foot," Sally said angrily. "What on earth are you talking about? And what happened to those loathsome Titanians that were here just a moment ago?"

"It worked!" they shouted in unison, and there was a great deal of hugging, backslapping and furtive knuckling of tears from eye corners. Once the hysterical moment was over they explained to Sally, in detail, what had happened. They had but one question, and Jerry phrased it for all of them.

"We have only one question. Why did you open the plane door and let the Titanians in?"

"They knocked three times, and you *told* me to open the door at three knocks. That's a foolish question," she sniffed, and they dared not disagree with her. "In any case it's nice that it all ended the way it did and all. And I'm really not sorry I missed most of it. Frankly I'm rather glad I was frozen by the time the Titanian king was caressing my limbs with his tentacles because I should not have liked that at all. So—when do we go back to Earth?"

"As soon as we have destroyed all of the disgusting carnivorous Garnishee," Jerry said stalwartly. "We can do at least that for these fine people here. And I must align the cheddite projector, and to do that I must find out where we are."

"This is the planet Domite which circles the star Proxima Centauri," Steigen-Sterben said, entering the operating room. "After dark you will be able to see the nearby double star of Alpha Centauri, the smaller companion of which is almost identical with the primary of your own solar system."

"He speaks pretty good English for a bald guy with four arms," Sally said, impressed.

"Steigen-Sterben at your service, dear Miss Sally. It is a pleasure to have you among us in revived form. Now, Mr. Jerry, if I could be so bold as to ask you about the weapon you had proposed constructing that would destroy once and for all our disgusting enemies. Is it ready?"

"It will be as soon as we have built a vacuum chamber. Sooner or later we will have to use the cheddite projector in an atmosphere, so it might as well be sooner. If we build it into a portable vacuum chamber, I will show you how this miracle of transportation can also be used as a humane weapon to end your millennia-old war once and for all."

"All our facilities, needless to say, are completely at your disposal."

While Sally went to make herself some new clothes to replace the torn summer frock she had been frozen in, the three companions brought the cheddite projector from the *Pleasantville Eagle* and labored to build it into a portable vacuum chamber. Or rather two of them did. Chuck stopped once to think and stood, deep in thought, for almost twenty minutes. He was in the way, so they stood him in the corner while they worked. Twenty minutes later, to the second, his eyes refocused, and he turned to them with grave tones.

"I hate to say it, but I think there is something slightly fishy about our four-armed friend Steigen-Sterben."

"Other than some strange eating habits," Jerry said, "I don't think there is anything wrong with old S-S."

"Then listen. If we are on a planet of the star Proxima Centauri—how far are we from Earth?"

"Four point three light-years," Jerry snapped back instantly. "Give or take a few miles."

"Check. Now when was the Pleasantville General Hospital and Rest Home built?"

57

"Two years ago . . . but . . . of course! We've been tricked!"

"I don't dig you, man," John said sourly.

"It's obvious. Steigen-Sterben said he heard about the hospital from a radio broadcast. Yet since radio waves disperse at the speed of light, the broadcast about the hospital will not arrive here for over *two years more!*"

"I admit to a slight deception, ha-ha, but it was only done in the name of friendship," Steigen-Sterben said, slipping into the room and smiling his toothless grin at them. The grin faded when the three men closed in on him, fists clenched.

"You lied to us," Jerry snapped out. "You are a mind reader, aren't you?"

"Just a little," he admitted, raising his four hands palms outward, while shrinking back at the same time. "Please let me explain. I meant no harm. We have simple mental powers of perception, being able to read surface thoughts, but not deeply. I saw that a creature on the moon you just left knew your language from radio broadcasts, so foolishly, I said that, feeling you would not like to have your minds read. Yes, I read in your minds now that you do not like having your minds read. So I will stop. I lied only for the greater cause of freedom."

"We can't beat up on him for that, I guess," Jerry said, lowering his fist, as did the others. "So I guess we'll have to go along with him." He turned and shook his finger at Steigen-Sterben. "But no mind reading without permission, do you hear? We like a bit of privacy."

Steigen-Sterben looked at him in puzzlement. "Why do you shake your finger at me?" he asked. "I do not know what you say since I am not reading your mind."

"You're an honest old coot," Jerry said shaking his hand, and Chuck and John shook his hand too at the same time, which they could do and even have one left over. Jerry tapped his head and pointed at the puzzled Ormoloo, who finally understood and read his mind.

"Very happy that peace is restored," he smiled toothlessly. "From now on I shall only read your minds when you tap on the side of your head like that. In such manner

58

will communication be established and privacy maintained. Now tell me—is this device you are constructing completed yet?"

"Just about to try it out." Chuck waved. "The tank is evacuated and the cheddite projector aligned. Now I set the controls on the outside of the tank." He did so, squinting through the open window at the mountain range nearby. "They're all ready. A push of the button will activate it and I leave that up to you, S-S, you four-armed, bald, toothless, friendly old coot."

"I will be grateful for eternity. But what will happen?"

"Just look at the mountains and press."

He did, and blinked quickly. "Am I having eye trouble or did I just see a forty-five-thousand-foot snowcapped mountain peak vanish completely?"

"You're not just snapping your mouth bones!" Jerry chortled. "The explanation is extremely simple. That mountain peak was enveloped by the kappa radiation and slipped into the lambda dimension and dropped out of the lambda dimension right over the middle of that big ocean back there. I'll bet the fish were surprised!"

"I'll bet the Garnishee will be surprised when *they* drop into that ocean." He grinned, and they all laughed together, but suddenly Steigen-Sterben stopped laughing and rushed toward the door.

"What's up?" Chuck called after him.

"A surprise attack by the Garnishee! They approach in force." And then he was gone.

"Well, there's something *we* can do about this, guys," Jerry said. "Let's load the cheddite projector onto this wagon and take it up to the walls."

They jumped to it, and just in time too. When they reached the courtyard of the fort, Sally had just run through the gate, which was slammed behind her almost in the teeth of the attacking Garnishee.

"I saw them just in time," she said breathlessly. "I ran every foot of the way back from the plane. What do you think of my outfit?"

She was tastefully dressed in neat shorts and blouse of colorful fabric cut from the Pleasantville football uniforms. But she had to stamp her foot in annoyance—how like men!—as they did not even answer her but ran quickly away staggering under the weight of a big tank thing. Men! Always thinking of themselves and not even answering a civil question!

While the Earthmen set up their projector, the Ormoloo were fighting for their very lives, for this was an attack in force with hundreds of armored vehicles streaking down from the hills. On the parapet nearby a linear magnetic projector was hard at work. The slaving Ormoloo loaded tar ball after tar ball into the breech of the weapon, inserting a fuse just before firing. Iron filings were mixed with the tar, and these particles of iron were clutched inexorably by the powerful magnetic field and flashed through the rings of the barrel, faster and faster, before being hurled out of the muzzle. When these tar balls struck they stuck, then ignited and burned with a fierce flame visible even in the full daylight. Nor was this the only weapon the Ormoloo used. They had a catapult with two large arms in the shape of a Y to which were fastened a rubberlike material that was stretched back by the laboring soldiers. When it was stretched to the utmost, a bomb with sputtering fuse was loaded into the leather seat, and the whole was released with devastating effect. In addition, they had cannon and rifles, not unlike their earthly counterparts, which they used with deadly effect upon the enemy. Who still charged closer, relying on their numbers to crush and capture the fort.

"Ready," Jerry shouted.

"Hurry," a nearby gunner called out. "For they are at our very gates and we are lost if their reserves arrive."

"Well, *that* for the reserves," Jerry muttered and pressed the activating switch.

Instantly, with a motion too fast for the eye to see, an entire attacking battalion of armored vehicles winked out of existence. Their tracks were still on the ground—ending abruptly—and the cloud of dust raised by their passage still hung in the air. But they were gone! A cheer broke out from the defenders.

"If you listen closely, you can hear the splashes," Jerry shouted, and they laughed in unison.

The rest of the attackers went the way of the first and the battle was won. While victory still enthused them, they loaded the cheddite projector into the *Pleasantville Eagle*, repaired the hole in the wing, and filled the tanks with fuel from the Ormoloo vehicles which proved to have very much the chemical composition of aviation jet fuel. Soon they were climbing into the sky, following the pointing finger of Steigen-Sterben, who went along as their guide.

"That direction," he said. "It will not be necessary for you to go below the clouds, in which case your magnificent air vessel would risk being shot down. I am in touch by mental telepathy with our observers in the front lines, and they inform me of our exact position. I will tell you when you are over the enemy lines—get ready—an immense fort below us that has stopped our advance for two thousand years—*now!*" The button was pressed. "Ahh, no more fort. If you will be ready, forty thousand troops massed for the attack . . . *now!*"

And so it went. Before the day was out Jerry's thumb was tired from pressing the button on the cheddite projector and Chuck had to relieve him at the controls. By late afternoon they were low on fuel and had to turn back but, meanwhile, they had destroyed most of the opposing army of the enemy, and the war, after ten thousand years, was won for the Ormoloo. There was indeed jubilation and a banquet waiting for them when they landed.

"I don't think I could take another of those banquets," John whispered to the others when Steigen-Sterben was out of earshot inspecting the toilet facilities of the 747.

"Me too," Jerry agreed.

"And I'll put in my vote," Chuck added. "Particularly, when you get down to it, since we haven't eaten for something like four days now, nor have we had much sleep."

"That's true," Jerry told him. "But we've been busy. When we get back, we'll ask Sally, who is waiting in our quarters in the fort, to rustle up something for us."

"What?" John muttered hungrily. "There's no food in the plane and only grass for the Ormoloo."

61

"Don't worry," Jerry said cheerily. "She'll think of something. She's a darn clever cook."

They swooped in for a landing just before sunset and trooped into the fort.

"See you at the celebration in a while, Steigen-Sterben," Jerry said. "We're going to see what Sally can rustle up for us."

"Of course, but do not be late, for this is the greatest moment in ten thousand years of history of our poor planet. Your names will ring down through the ages."

"Nix on that," Jerry told him, and the others nodded agreement. "We can't take that kind of thing. We're just some guys doing our job and helping our friends and we don't go for that sort of mush, no, sir!"

They tramped through the halls and through the open door and called out the name of the girl whom at least two of them loved.

"Sally!"

Her piercing scream was the only answer. They fought each other to be first through the door and entered just in time to see her shrieking body being carried in the tentacles of a stinking Garnishee down through a secret trapdoor let into the floor. They dived forward as one, only to have the trapdoor slam shut in their faces. Cursing and struggling, they tore at the unyielding metal, and Steigen-Sterben ran breathlessly into the room.

"I heard your mental cries of anger and fear," he said, "so I came at once."

"Sally," Chuck panted, "that *thing* took her down there. Help us get this trapdoor open, so we can follow and save her."

Steigen-Sterben's forehead wrinkled with intense thought, and then he sighed a deep and tremulous sigh. With a despairing gesture he reached out and laid a comforting hand on the shoulder of all three of them and made a helpless gesture with his remaining hand.

"Struggle no more, I beg of you," he entreated.

"Why?" struggling, "we must save her."

"You cannot," Steigen-Sterben intoned in the most funereal of tones. "For it is too late. I attempted to reach

her mind with mine to enable you to locate her when—
pfiff—with utmost suddenness her thoughts were no
more."

"You mean. . . ."

"Sadly, I do. If her thoughts have been stopped this
poor girl, so far from home, is dead."

8

THE GHASTLY SECRET
REVEALED

The shocked silence continued for an inordinately long time because, as you can very well imagine, no one had much to say after receiving *that* news. Steigen-Sterben, knowing how they felt, tiptoed out of the door and left them to their sadness.

"She was a good old girl," Chuck finally choked out.

"A-number-one," Jerry choked in answer.

"Let's go fuel up the plane and rebuild that starboard engine," Jerry suggested.

"Good idea," Chuck agreed, and they left in silence with their misery.

John let them go, knowing they wanted to be alone together, or maybe just alone, or maybe together, with their loss. He felt the loss no less keenly himself, although he had known that wonderful girl only from a distance up until a few days ago. He scuffled about the room dazedly, and when he passed the sealed trapdoor, he gave it a vicious kick and it instantly flew open. At this unexpected event he drew back, his keen senses alert again, wondering instantly what it could mean. Whatever it meant he had to investigate, even if the dark opening were filled with repellent Garnishee—in fact, he would welcome that! Take as many as possible to the grave with him. He remembered that there was an armory in the next room, and he hurried there and seized a heavy sword, then rushed back to the gaping entrance to the netherworld revealed by the open trapdoor. Filled by conflicting emotions, he did not think or reason but hurled himself headlong into the darkness.

Something struck his skull heavily, and he was unconscious on the instant.

When he came to an immeasurable period of time later,

all was in darkness still, and his head hurt. Not only that but there was an awful stench in the air, and he knew instantly that it was the Garnishee, he had heard they smelled bad and, wow!, was that rumor ever right. They were close around him, unseen and slithering close, and the instant a wet tentacle slithered down his face, he lashed out with a quick fist and connected solidly, and a really satisfying scream—they screamed like girls—was his reward.

Then there was a sudden flare of light, and he saw that he had been right and he was surrounded by the repulsive Garnishee. Well, half right at least, because the one he had hit was really Sally Goodfellow, who had been stroking his head, who, in return, got a right cross to the eye, which was now producing a really interesting mouse.

"You're alive!" he gasped.

"No thanks to you, you monster! You trying to kill me?"

"I thought you were a monster."

"Well, you thought wrong, and gee, thanks."

"We thought you were dead. Steigen-Sterben told us so."

"Old Steigy has said a lot of things that aren't so kosher. Now listen. . . ."

"You listen. I just found out that I am sitting on my sword. When I count to three, you make a break for it, and I'll cut these creeps down. One, two—"

"No, hold on, will you, and just listen for a minute." She dived across the intervening space and hung from his sword arm so he couldn't lift it, and two of the Garnishee quickly disarmed him.

"Why, you ofay dyke, traitor to the human race and—"

"I said listen, not flap the jaw. Listen and learn."

"Weel you tell heem all?" the Garnishee who was holding the lamp said, disconcertingly, because his mouth was just above his waist, where, if he were a human being, he would have had his *pippick*.

"I'll tell him, Slug-Togath, but make sure your boys hold onto him well. One shiner a day is enough."

"Why, you—"

"Shaddap. Listen and learn, kiddo. We have been had. Steigen-Sterben and his bunch are nothing but a bunch of weirdos who have been trying to take over this planet for ten thousand years from the law-abiding Garnishee."

"Who fed you this line of guff?"

"I did, young man," said Slug-Togath, "so please have the courtesy to permit the young lady to finish before you interrupt."

"Yeah," John sneered, feeling put down, "Your manners aren't so great either, nor is your smell. And your English isn't so wonderful. Where did you learn it, on the radio?"

"It so happens I did. Our powerful receivers have been listening to your radio programs for years. *Little Orphan Annie*, BBC, Radio Free Transylvania, *Buck Rogers*, Radio Moscow, the works. Though you apparently have received none of our answering broadcasts, undoubtedly because of the inferiority of your receivers."

Feeling more than a little put upon, John relaxed, although the imprisoning tentacles held firm, and then listened with growing incredulity.

"First off," Sally explained, "the Garnishee grabbed me and then hit you on the head in the darkness so that the Ormoloo, who monitor our thoughts all the time no matter what you hear to the contrary, would think I had been killed. What really happened was they put a mind shield on my head, your head too, so our thoughts could not be read. See mine." She turned so he could see the golden mesh of wire on her skull, very much like an alien yarmulke, and he became aware, at the same time, of one on his own head as well.

"Once my mind was shielded Slug-Togath explained, with colored slides, the history of this planet. It seems the Garnishee are the only intelligent race here, and since they are millennia older than our Earth civilizations, they are way ahead of us in the science field and that kind of thing. They have a democratic form of government with an elected head of state, that's Slug-Togath here, he is the prime minister, a two-house congress, a supreme court and graduated income tax. All was like unto a paradise on

66

Earth, or rather Domite, until the Lortonoi came along and began this war of extinction."

"The *who?*"

"The Lortonoi."

"That's what I thought you said. But what about the Ormoloo, whom they are supposed to be fighting?"

"They are nothing but domesticated animals, like cattle on Earth, whose minds, what they have of them, have been seized by the Lortonoi and have been used for their evil ends."

"Well, that at least explains their eating habits—and that film we saw!"

"I heard about that. That film was made by the Garnishee many years ago. It's a training film for a butcher's school, showing how to cut the Ormoloo up for chops and steaks and things like that. Now shut up and listen, will you, because we don't have too much time. Where was I? Oh, yes, ten thousand years ago the Lortonoi landed on this planet and attempted to seize the minds of the Garnishee and turn them into slaves so they could use the advanced technology here since they, the Lortonoi, have never had any science of their own but only use slave races to do everything. Anyway, the Garnishee resisted, and some unsung genius invented the mind shields which they now all wear from the moment of birth."

"How can they?" John broke in, becoming more confused instead of less. "They don't have heads but tentacles on top instead."

"They can because they wear the mind shields on their brains, not their heads, stupid, so they don't need heads. Particularly since they have their brains in one of their feet." And sure enough, now that his attention was drawn to it, John saw that each of the aliens had a mind shield on one foot. "So once their minds were shielded they fought back and determined to crush the evil invaders. But this has taken a long time. From their secret headquarters the Lortonoi fiends took control of many of the Ormoloo, causing them to break free of the ranches and fields, to kill the cowboys, and to rise against their masters. By themselves the Ormoloo have the intelligence of retarded

67

sheep, but their minds are now controlled from afar, so they organize into armies, run factories and that kind of thing, and war to the death against the peaceful Garnishee."

It took John a few minutes to digest this, but digest it he did, and his jaw firmed up, and he reached a decision.

"It all makes sense, Sally, and if it is true, then we'd better rush and get hold of Jerry and Chuck because they are in great danger because I am sure that all the Ormoloo want from us is the secret of the cheddite projector. But I must have some *proof*. I cannot take this all on hearsay, as, you will pardon my saying so, you have. It is one thing to convince a simple, though lovely, girl—"

"Why, thanks a lot, buster! I have a BA in home economics!"

"—it is another thing to show proof to someone of my background and training in spying, warfare, intelligence, brain surgery, proctoscopy, codes and ciphers, blue-ribbon cooking, and murder."

Tentacles waved, and Slug-Togath waved fastest. "Waving tentacles mean agreement, tovarich—or is it mister?" he said.

"Call me John—but that's only for my friends."

"We desperately desire your friendship soon-to-be-called-John. Come this way, for demonstration has been prepared."

He led the way through a labyrinth of tunnels that apparently lay under the Ormoloo fort, to a dimly lit room one wall of which was made of glass.

"Silence," he whispered, "for we can be heard but not seen since that partition is made of one-way glass. If you will look, you will see some Ormoloo whom we have recently taken prisoner."

John looked and gasped. The Ormoloo were down on all sixes, or rather what he thought had been arms had really been legs, which explained the variations in joints he had noticed. They strolled about with empty stares while some of their number ate grass from a manger. One of them mooed lowingly, and the others took up the cry until it sounded like milking time on the ranch.

"But what?" John gasped.

"Look," Slug-Togath directed. "Each of them is wearing a mind shield so it cannot be controlled by the Lortonoi. Now the demonstration. We have a remote manipulating apparatus in the ceiling with which we will remove the brain shield from any of these creatures that you may select. The choice is up to you."

"You're on. Okay, that one there that's making like feeding time at the zoo."

A metal arm tipped with claw fingers dropped down from above and whisked the shielding from the Ormoloo's head. Instantly it spat out the grass and stood upright on its hind legs, the light of evil intelligence now glowing in its formerly bucolic eyes. There was a rack of swords across the room, and it dived that way and seized one. Instantly Slug-Togath spoke.

"Put down that sword and surrender. If you don't, we will injure that Ormoloo body you have possessed." His only answer was an evil cackle.

"What care I for this cattle body?" the thing shouted and leaped forward sword raised. "We Lortonoi cannot die, but you Garnishee can, and we will not stop until you are destroyed. . . ."

The metal arm swooped and put the mind shield back into place and instantly a dramatic change took place. The sword clattered to the floor, and the Ormoloo dropped back on all sixes, mooing loudly, then returned to the grass and began to feed again. John had seen enough.

"Slug-Togath, old monster, I have seen enough," he said. "Put her there." And they shook hands, or rather tentacles, or rather *tentacle* and *hand*. "From now on we're on the same side. Now let's go get the rest of the gang."

"Might I suggest that discretion is the better part of valor," Slug-Togath suggested. "If it is discovered that you are using mind shields, you will instantly have every Ormoloo turned against you. What is important, and the first order of business, is to grab the cheddite projector. Once you have that secured we will pour out of the tunnels and overwhelm the fort, and you will be safe, as will the *Pleas-*

antville Eagle. We will have only this one chance, and we must not muff it, because all our surviving warriors are here in the tunnel, only cripples and children remain at home, since you annihilated ninety-nine point nine percent of our people."

"Sorry about that."

"Not half as sorry as we are, but that is neither here nor there, and within a thousand years our population will have grown again. But now, to work! Darkness has fallen, and we will lead you through this maze of tunnels to an exit very near your flying vehicle. Remember, to the Lortonoi you are invisible since your mind is shielded. But if one of their slave Ormoloo sees you that will be the ball game. So—steal home and hit a home run."

"You hear a lot of baseball games on your high-powered radio?"

"Far too many. Now go! Take these mind shields for your friends, and place this communicating device in your pocket, and once you have the cheddite projector in your possession, press this button labeled *apritzxer* which can be translated, roughly, as OK."

"I can't read these hen tracks."

"Most annoying. Well, this one then, of the color red."

"You're on."

"Good luck!" Sally called out. "The fate of a world, perhaps of the whole known universe, rests with you."

He pressed her hand, then was gone. The Garnishee stumped quickly along on their thick legs, and he had to hurry to keep up. Finally they came to a tunnel that ended in a raw dirt wall.

"Extinguish the lights," Slug-Togath ordered. "We have arrived. Only a foot of dirt remains between us and the surface. My men will now dig it away, and you will emerge. Our hopes go with you."

There was a rapid insufflating sound, and an opening appeared in the raw dirt and was quickly widened. Stars were visible in the dark sky beyond, and aided by a pushing tentacle, John squeezed through and onto the ground beyond. He was in a shallow gully, and when he peered carefully over the edge, he saw the fort, illuminated

70

in the darkness, with the *Pleasantville Eagle* close by. He crawled that way, seeking what cover he could, drawn on by the welcoming cabin lights. He smiled into the darkness, knowing what kind of welcome his news would bring. Sally alive! What a greeting he would get! Then the gangway was close to hand, and after a quick look around to make sure that the coast was clear, he rushed up it and into the cabin. The door opened to the pilot's compartment, and Chuck came in carrying the cheddite projector.

"Chuck!" John called out. "I have some really tremendous news for you. But first put down that gadget because I don't want it busted."

"Yes," Chuck said, listlessly, undoubtedly still filled with grief about Sally. Was he in for a surprise!

"Now listen, guy—and I'm really on the level. About Sally . . . what are you doing?"

He looked on puzzledly as Chuck straightened up again with the submachine gun in his arms, an evil grin on his features.

"What am I going to do? I am going to kill you, filthy alien swine!"

The gun roared point blank, and darkness instantly fell.

9

THE LAST BATTLE—
OR IS IT?

After an unmeasurable amount of time John crept feebly back to consciousness. His head felt as though it had been caught in a destruction derby, and for quite a while, all he could do was lie there quietly and not even moan because even moaning hurt. Finally, with great reluctance he forced one eye open, then the other, and discovered that he was lying in the aisle of the plane staring up at the ceiling. Hesitantly he raised reluctant fingers to his bruised skull and touched it, which did not feel nice at all, and brought them away bloodstained. Shot to death! was his first thought, but, since he was still alive and not paralyzed, he realized that was not true. It appeared that one bullet at least had grazed his skull, he hoped without fracturing it, and had rendered him unconscious.

Bullet! When he realized what this meant full memory returned in a flash, and he groped, groaning, for the communicator from his pocket. For some unfathomable reason Chuck had shot him and escaped with the cheddite projector. The red button meant OK, so he stayed away from that one and played a tune of despair upon all the others since things definitely were not OK.

A shrill squeaking sound and a guttural growl reached his ears, and instantly, despite the triphammer of pain it produced in his head, he was on his feet and facing this new menace, hands outstretched in the judo killer position. The eerie sounds were coming from the direction of the control cabin, so crouched in the judo defense position, he stalked there on wary tiptoes, ready for anything. Though he lowered his guard, settled onto his heels, and gaped when he saw what it was that had disturbed him.

Jerry Courteney lay on the cabin floor writhing like a snake. He was on his back, his eyes closed, his fists clenched, growling like a dog, and gritting his teeth at the same time to make the chalk-on-blackboard squeaking sound. For a long moment John gazed at his writhing friend in wide-eyed astonishment, then, through the tortured synapses of his beat-up brain came the first glimmerings of understanding.

"The Lortonoi, who else!" he ejaculated, then groped in his pocket for one of the mind shields the Garnishee had given him. Kneeling, he slipped it into place on Jerry's head. The results were incredibly dramatic. Jerry instantly stopped writhing and growling, and his body relaxed, and he opened his eyes and smiled.

"Wow," he breathed, "gone at last."

"Was *something* trying to get into your mind and control you?" John queried.

"Brother, you are not just whistling 'Dixie'! Insidious mental tentacles of some hideously repulsive alien life form were attempting to take over my body—but I fought back! The hardest battle of my entire career. I couldn't throw them out, and finally, they must have decided they could not win because they settled for just dropping me down on the deck and closing my eyes. I was struggling away when all of a sudden they left, poof, just like that!"

"The mind shield. I put it on your head so they couldn't get through to you."

"That's pretty good, John. You wouldn't like to tell me where you got a gadget like that, would you?"

"It's a long story but first—"

"Death to the aliens!" Jerry shouted, leaping to his feet. "Three cheers for the red, white, and blue!" He seized up the oxyhydrogen torch, lit it to flaring life and dived to the attack toward the Garnishee who were crowding into the cabin. John gave him a quick karate chop to the wrist as he went by, so the torch dropped, then another quick hack on the kidneys, which paralyzed him and dropped him back to the deck again.

"Traitor!" Jerry growled at John when he knelt to turn

off the torch and struggled to raise his hands to throttle his former companion. Two more lightning karate chops paralyzed his arms as well, so John could reason with him.

"It's a complicated story, I tried to tell you, but part of it is *good,* like look there, see who has come to take care of you."

"Sally! Alive!" Jerry gasped as the girl pushed through the tentacles and hurried to his side. "It is indeed a miracle."

Her tender arms embraced him, and they kissed, and John writhed like a willow in the wind burned by the hot fires of jealousy, for he too, now, had to admit that, like the others, he was head over heels in love with this slim girl. He forced his eyes away from this painful necking scene and faced Slug-Togath, who had led his noisome followers as they crowded into the plane.

"Here is what I think happened," John told the alien prime minister. "The Lortonoi must have been very suspicious when Sally and I both 'vanished' mentally, and they may have gotten their wind up and had a bug in their ear."

"What do their digestion and their hearing have to do with it?" Slug-Togath asked in puzzlement.

"Will you kindly shut up and let me finish? Fearing that their dark secret had been discovered, they launched a mental attack on Chuck and Jerry here in the plane. Jerry fought back with every fiber of his being, and the most they could do was hold him down mentally while they worked their plan. But, somehow, they took over Chuck's brain. They made him grab the cheddite projector and light out of here on the double. That's when I showed up, so they made him shoot me, or at least try to. He is a crack shot, so I should be dead, but since I am not, it seems he still has a measure of control and was able to deflect their aim. Once I went down he escaped with the cheddite projector and, if you will pardon my saying so, shouldn't we be taking off after him instead of standing around beating our gums?"

There was a thunder of heavy feet as the Garnishee rushed for the door. Slug-Togath stayed behind and issued incomprehensible orders in a strange tongue through a hand communicator.

"The attack has begun," he announced. "We have hurled our entire remaining forces against the fort. Pray to Great Cacodyl that we succeed before their reinforcements arrive."

"Let me shake your tentacle," Jerry said, now recovered, striding forward. "Sally has told me everything, and I'm glad to have you on our side. I'm sorry about, you know, wiping out almost all your ancient and intelligent race . . ."

"Fortunes of war, we shall not speak of it again. Ahh, I have a message!" The communicator blurbled and bleeped. "The walls have been breached, we are inside the fort, the attack is succeeding, though, of course, not without an incredible loss of life on both sides. Wait! What is this? Something has happened. The advance guard reports a hideous alien life form has been spotted—that must be your friend, Chuck—they are closing in but *preprabish-kom!* he is escaping!"

They rushed to the windows and had their first view of the battle. Half the fort was in ruins, and flames guttered through the rest. Bodies, of friend and foe alike, littered the landscape, which was also a junkyard of wrecked war vehicles.

"There he goes!" Slug-Togath shouted, pointing a quivering tentacle.

From the ruined fort there slowly rose up a strange flying vehicle. Shells exploded around it, but miraculously, it escaped and rose even higher in the merciless glare of the piercing Garnishee searchlights. It was a steam-driven ornithopter held aloft by four pairs of great flapping black wings. Smoke gushed from the chimney, and the wings thrashed and beat strongly as the flying machine gathered speed and rushed toward the horizon.

"Strap in, everyone," Jerry shouted, diving for the controls. "We're going after him!"

They barely had time to find their seats before the great bulk of the *Pleasantville Eagle* was roaring down the improvised runway and hurling itself into the air.

"I have it on the radar," John announced. "It looks like he's heading due north."

"I feared that," Slug-Togath said gloomily, but would not elucidate.

"We'll catch up with them quickly enough," Jerry said assuredly. "That wing-flapping gadget can't outfly this baby."

But Jerry's prediction was brought to naught, for as soon as the ornithopter had reached sufficient altitude and speed, a built-in ramjet fired, and the wings were retracted, and the now jet-powered aircraft sizzled north above the speed of sound. It was all that the 747 could do, throttles wide open, to keep the alien vessel on the edge of the radarscope.

"They have to come down some time," Jerry said, grimly. "And when they do, we'll be there."

Onwards they raced in this race to save a race, a man, a world, possibly the entire inhabited galaxy, and soon dawn rushed upon them and, yes, their quarry was visible as a dark spot against the eternal snowfields that hurtled by below.

"What in tarnation is he doing up here at the North Pole?" Jerry asked puzzledly. "Does anyone live up here?"

"Not to our knowledge," Slug-Togath answered grimly. "But we have our suspicions. It seems that during all the centuries of eternal warfare upon this planet we have never known where the secret base is from which the Lortonoi operate with their mental powers. We have had suspicions and have raided certain areas, but we feel now that these were, how do you say it, blue herrings to throw us off—"

"Red," Jerry said. "We say *red.*"

"Blue reds to throw us off—"

"*Herrings,* not *reds,* you got it wrong—"

"Look, do you mind if I finish the story and we save the goddamn language lesson for later?" Slug-Togath snapped irritably, undoubtedly fatigued and out of sorts because of the destruction of most of his millennia-old race. "For the last few centuries we have come to suspect one certain inaccessible location at the North Pole, an extinct volcano named Mount Krisco, and plans were being drawn up for a secret attack."

"The escaping ornithopter-jet is losing speed and dropping!" John called out, hunched over the radar screen. "It's going down, and it looks like it is heading toward that mountain, the big one that looks like an extinct volcano."

"Mount Krisco." Slug-Togath sighed.

"Is he committing suicide?" Sally screeched as the ornithopter-jet dived straight at the side of the mountain.

"Would he were," Slug-Togath intoned grimly. "I realize you will be put out by the death of your friend, but this is as nothing to one who has lost almost his entire race, and it would mean the destruction of the cheddite projector which would keep it out of the hands—if they have hands—of the Lortonoi. No, too bad, such a happy course is not possible."

At the very last instant a great slab of the solid mountain swung back to reveal a black opening in the stone cliff. The 747 dived to follow, but long before they were close, the secret entrance had closed again so that they had to veer off.

"I'll land on that ice sheet there," Jerry said. "We'll follow him into the secret hideout."

Meanwhile, Sally, who was more than a little rumpled after being kidnapped, dragged through tunnels and that kind of thing, decided she ought to freshen up or at least comb the tangles out of her hair. Unthinkingly she picked up her comb and took the mind shield from her head. Instantly, she was a different person. A look of malevolent cunning swept across her features and painted them with an evil grin while her tongue darted in and out like a snake's. With her fingers clenching and unclenching like talons she sidled across the cabin and, in a lightning-quick motion seized the submachine gun and flicked off the safety.

"This is the end for all of you," she snarled in a voice rich with venom. "Look upon your deaths, and let me revel in your expressions of horrified shock before I press the trigger and send this plane with all aboard crashing into the Artic wastes."

77

"Sally—have you gone mad?" Jerry cried out, flicking on the automatic pilot and jumping to his feet.

"No!" Slug-Togath called out and put out a tentacle to stop him. "That is not Sally talking. I recognize the voice as one of the Lortonoi. She must have lost her mind shield."

"Very acute thinking, Garnishee swine." Sally laughed in the alien voice of the *thing* that had possessed her. "But soon you will think no more. We now have the secret of the cheddite projector and no longer need waste our time on your backward planet. The galaxy is ours!"

With these last shouted words she pressed hard on the trigger, and ravening bullets screamed from the muzzle of the gun. But quick as she had been, Slug-Togath was quicker. He hurled his trunklike body into the path of the bullets, then tore the weapon from her hand, imprisoning her instantly with many tentacles.

"You're hurt," Jerry called out. "Shot a dozen times at least!"

"Please do not concern yourself for my physical condition. We Garnishee are very tough and almost bulletproof, and the few slugs that penetrated will be absorbed by my body chemistry in a matter of days."

"Too late, too late!" Sally rasped in a hoarse voice and began to laugh madly.

"What does she, I mean it, mean?"

"There is your answer," Slug-Togath pointed. "The Lortonoi are fleeing our planet, escaping with the galaxy's most important secret."

Even as he spoke, there was a rumble from the extinct volcano and a flare of fire and a plume of smoke. But this was no simple eruption, a plain matter of lava and poison gas, but something far more important. With a thunderous roar a great spaceship hurled itself into the air from the mouth of the volcano and sped skyward. Faster and faster it went, shrinking to a tiny dot and then finally vanishing completely.

"They have escaped," Slug-Togath sighed, and his tentacles went limp. Sally dropped to the floor, and John put her mind shield back on.

78

"Well, let's not worry too much, gang," Jerry said, looking for the bright side of the disaster. "They won't hurt Chuck, not as long as he is of value to them, and we'll go after them and get him back safe and sound, just you wait and see."

"How will you do that?" Slug-Togath asked.

"Simplicity itself. The old *Pleasantville Eagle* here is a tough old bird and already has logged a lot of hours in space. We'll fix her up for operation in a vacuum, as well as atmosphere, slap together another cheddite projector and go after him."

"A really great idea," John said raising one eyebrow sardonically. "But just how are you going to go about building this projector?"

"Well. First get some cheddar cheese and put it into . . ." His voice ran down like a tired phonograph record, and he gaped into silence.

"Good thinking, old buddy," John said, still sardonically. "All we need is a hunk of cheese to build the projector, a certain kind of cheese. But that cheese is back on Earth, and in order to get to Earth we are going to need a projector that we need the cheese for, or do you read me? In my humble American-German-Russian opinion we are up the creek without a paddle."

10

AN INSIDE JOB AND
A NOBLE CRUSADE

It was one of those moments about which it might have
been said that the emotional tenor of those present bor-
dered on the abysmally depressed. It *might* have been
said. It could not have been said because where there is
hope, there is life, and Jerry, shocked as he was by this
disclosure, still had hope, and he sent his agile mind furiously seeking a solution to this apparently insoluble
problem. In the matter of seconds he had it.

"Hold on now," he said, snapping his fingers loudly. "I
remember something. When we originally left on this trip,
we thought we would be away at least a couple of hours,
ha-ha, little did we know, and I have memories of Chuck
fixing up some sandwiches to take along just in case."

"What *kind* of sandwiches?" John entreated in hushed
tones.

"That's a mystery. I remember he just went out and
made them. But knowing old Chuck, now a mental prisoner of those fiends but still a buddy, I know they were
one of two kinds. Either garlic salami or cheddar cheese."

"I don't see us building a garlicite projector," John
mused. "But *if* they were cheese and *if* they weren't eaten
—why, we still have a chance. Let's go look in the galley!"

He led the race through the immense ship and skidded
to a halt with the others right behind him at the 747's galley. Sally, whom they had not noticed leave, was standing
by the counter licking crumbs from her fingers. Before her
on the counter was some crunkled wax paper.

"Stale and pretty lousy," she complained, and belched
delicately. "But when you consider we have been a week
now without food, I guess it wasn't too bad."

"You ate a *sandwich?*" Jerry rasped, and she nodded in response. "You ate the *whole* thing?" A nod again, then silence until John spoke up in a strangled voice.

"What *kind* of sandwich?"

"Cheese. What else would be here? My goodness, I don't know how Chuck ever managed to eat so much of it, it really is kind of nasty. Why are you all looking at me that way and closing in slowly? So, I'm sorry. I didn't save any for you. But I was hungry, I mean. . . ."

Her voice ran down under the glare of the circling eyes, and she took a hesitant step backward.

"Come on, fellows." She smiled falsely. "*One* little sandwich can't make *that* much difference."

"That little sandwich," John said, speaking for them all, "contained the only piece of cheddar cheese inside four light-years that could be used to make cheddite, with which we could save the galaxy. Do you realize what you have done?"

"Don't try to pass on the guilt to me," she snorted and fluffed her hair prettily with one hand. "It was just some old cheese, and if we don't save the galaxy, then someone else will. Besides, it is late to do anything about it now."

"No, it's not," John said coldly, unlocking the medical kit from the wall. "As a trained surgeon I can see one solution to our problem if we work quickly before the stomach acids. . . ."

"*No!*" she screamed when she saw the rubber tubing, and she tried to run but was entangled at once by the many tentacles of Slug-Togath, who held her immobile despite her struggles while the two Earthmen unshipped the stomach pump and went to work.

Good taste forbids depicting what follows, but it suffices to say that a few hours later we find the *Pleasantville Eagle* winging its way toward the secret underground city of the Garnishee with Jerry at the controls under the guidance of Slug-Togath who overflowed the copilot's seat. Everyone was happy, except Sally who, good little sport that she was, was not feeling too sporty this time, but a couple of miniatures of vodka on a very empty stomach had put

81

her to sleep, and she was sleeping comfortably in the lounge. It was at this moment that John popped into the pilot's compartment waving a test tube joyfully.

"All done, guys. The particles of cheese have all been extracted and cleaned and are in this tube. We now have the raw material for a cheddite projector."

"Raw is the word for it," Jerry mused. "How is Sally taking it all now?"

"The booze helped, and she is sacked out. But, my, what she called me before she dozed off. Where does a sweet little small-town girl whose daddy is president of the college get a vocabulary like that?"

"Evil companions, I guess. All those grunts back from Nam with their grass and filthy language, lousing up our campuses. Though I heard a really good one from this guy. It seems. . . ."

"Prepare to land," Slug-Togath said sharply, turning his body so one of his long-distance eyes could point straight ahead. "We are almost to the secret entrance."

"Secret is the word," Jerry muttered awedly. "There's nothing down there but sandy desert."

"Land now and taxi between those two mounds of rock," was the reply.

He did as instructed, and no sooner had the massive form of the *Pleasantville Eagle* come to a halt than they felt a sudden dropping motion. The desert here was nothing but a great elevator that lowered them swiftly deep into the ground. As they dropped, they saw the camouflaged roof close over them, and they kept on going down, faster and faster. Finally, they braked to a stop as the immense elevator dropped them into an immense cavern studded with lights above and filled with incomprehensible machinery.

"Ten thousand years ago our forefathers brought forth under this land a refuge for our civilization," Slug-Togath intoned proudly. "While the endless war was fought on the surface, down here in the darkness we preserved our cultural heritage. All our resources since that time have been spent in fighting the war, our industry producing only war machines, our mothers producing only warriors. But we have not forgotten. When our warriors become too old and shot up to fight, many of them retire here and work until they die, preserving this vital heritage. Dusting the books, polishing the glass, that kind of thing."

It was impressive beyond all comprehension. Giant machines of incomprehensible function rose up until they grew dim above. Great wheels, gears, glass envelopes containing incredible devices of unknown operation. And more and more of this, all separated by shelf after shelf of books printed on imperishable sheets of eternium metal.

"Do you have a particle accelerator down here?" Jerry asked.

"Let me consult with the head caretaker," Slug-Togath responded and approached an elderly Garnishee, whose tentacles were all gray and who wore eyepatches on at least half the eyes around his gnarled trunk. This individual waved his tentacles creakily in agreement and led the way down a broad corridor between the exhibits. Though they walked fast, it was a good half hour and they were feeling really pooped before they reached the device in question. Jerry and John took turns carrying Sally, and they were both staggering with exhaustion when they arrived and dropped onto the nearest bench.

"Though we are both crack athletes and in topnotch shape," Jerry said, "there is just one thing. Though we have had a good deal of water to drink, we have had no food, other than a mouthful of grass, in the past week. Sally is in the same shape, although she has at least seen a sandwich go by twice. So the big question is—is there anything we can eat?"

"There might be—but we must be very wary," Slug-Togath responded with trepidation. "Our proteins may be poison for you, and so forth. I suggest we take samples of your blood, sputum and krakkis—"

"Krakkis?" Jerry asked.

"Well, not krakkis maybe. I guess maybe only we Garnishee have krakkis. Let's have the other samples, and our topnotch scientists will bring you a report within minutes."

Not only did they bring a report within minutes but something even better: a wheeled table covered with a shining metal dome.

"Congratulations!" Slug-Togath reported. "Your vital fluids, other than your krakkis, check out to ten decimal points identical with those of the Garnishee. So what we eat you can eat, though you may not like it."

"What do you eat?" John asked, sniffing the air strongly.

"A simple peasant meal," Slug-Togath said, whipping the metal cover off the table. "Of prifl, torkootchy and korpsk," he intoned, pointing to a thick, medium-rare steak, baked potato, and black-eyed peas.

"I'll have a large prifl with torkootchy," Jerry said, seizing a long-tined fork. "And maybe the korpsk on the side."

He had to move fast to dodge the flying cutlery of his shipmates, and within seconds they were tucking into the banquet and stuffing themselves with yumms and mmmms of approval.

"My regards to the cook," Jerry mumbled without stopping chewing. "He does a great steak."

"He'll be glad to hear that," Slug-Togath rumbled pleasurably. "We have been pretty much vegetarians for years because the war used up most of the Ormoloo, but things are better now. We got a lot of chops and steaks out of the last battle."

The three Earthlings stopped eating for a moment and their eyes bulged as they realized they were eating their former allies, then enemies, now reduced back to their normal role of meat animals.

"It's as if we were fighting a war against Angus cows," Jerry explained, speaking for them all. "We wouldn't let all those steaks go to waste just because they were the enemy. And you know what happens to a bull after a bullfight."

Thus reassured, they dived in with a will and cleaned their plates under the benevolent and multiple eyes of their host. When the last scrap of food had been consumed, both John and Sally crapped out on the spot and began to snore. But not so Jerry, who knew his duty to rescue his comrade, so he staggered to his feet; besides, he had to find the head. It proved to be an interesting cubicle, and he couldn't figure out how *anything* really worked, but he did his best and emerged ready for work. In a matter of minutes the particle accelerator was fired up and calibrated and the ball of cheddar underwent the barrage that transformed it into a new form of matter. Jerry spared time for only one jubilant gaze before rushing to construct the necessary circuitry to activate the cheddite to generate the kappa radiation. Here the eons-old genius of the Garnishee came into play, and he was shown how to operate an incredible machine that constructed other machines from an outline of their functions drawn on a screen. In a matter of seconds it delivered a stronger, yet miniaturized version of the original cheddite projector—no bigger than an Earth flashlight. In fact, it looked very much like a five-cell flashlight with the cheddite mounted in the evacuated chamber with a glass cover just where the bulb would normally be. It could be mounted in delicate gimbals for distant work and could also be used as a hand weapon whisking anything it was pointed at into the lambda dimension, then depositing the whisked-away object one hundred feet above the surface of the nearby sun. A potent weapon indeed. The other two awoke, groaning, to a demonstration of the device.

"That's half the game." John eructated. "Now the *Pleasantville Eagle* must be prepared as a space vessel to continue the chase."

"Some work while others sleep!" Jerry chuckled. "Just come and look what the incredible Garnishee have done with their eons-old knowledge."

He led the way back to their plane, which looked superficially the same, though it had been polished to a high gloss. However, major changes had been made in the interior, not all of which were always visible to the naked eye.

"First off," explained Jerry, "the space between the inner and outer skin of the plane has been filled with insulite, which is a better insulater than a vacuum, I have been told. All the exterior windows are of transparent armolite, which is clear as glass and as strong as steel. We won't need oxygen for the engines, though there is now a supply for ourselves, since the fuel tanks are filled with combustite, a fuel a thousand times more powerful than our ordinary jet fuel and which does not need oxygen to burn. This is also used for powerful jets under the tail that may come in handy someday. All batteries have been replaced with ones made of Garnishee capacitite which seem to have unlimited capacity for storing electrical energy. Back here the galley has been expanded into a complete kitchen with hibachi and radar oven, and beyond it a frozen food locker that could feed us for five years if need be. Farther back is a completely outfitted laboratory and machine shop with stockpiles of raw ingredients. In this locker are extra-powerful spacesuits, each almost a small spaceship in itself, one for each of us and—gosh, I hope he uses it— one for Chuck as well." He hurried on so they would not hear the huskiness in his voice, but they heard it nevertheless and understood.

"Up here on top, the flight deck has been expanded right back to take over the entire first-class lounge; the bar's a deck below now, to hold all the new equipment and controls. This chair here is for the gunner because remote-controlled gun turrets have been installed in twelve positions and armed with rapid-fire weapons firing pellets filled with destructite, an explosive a thousand times more powerful than gunpowder."

He went on to point out the various controls and other devices far too numerous to mention, though he promised to later, but he did point out and take pride in one set of controls that filled an entire end of the compartment.

"I don't know if we will ever need this," he opined, "but the old *Eagle* has been equipped with a space drive, the same kind that the Lortonoi and everyone else in the galaxy use, the only kind of space drive that cut the mustard until the cheddite projector came down the pike and knocked it into a cocked hat. It's called a space warper."

"How does it work?" John queried.

"By warping space. There is a great projector source which projects a beam of energy through a disk of war-

86

pite. This produces a new form of radiation that emerges in the form of warpicles, not wavicles, and is sent blasting through space ahead of the ship. What it does is reach out and seize the very fabric of space itself and pull it toward the ship until there is a great bulge in space flattened out before the ship, which then flies through it as the warp is released so that it emerges on the far side of the bulge, which is maybe a light year or so ahead. Clear?"

"Clear!" John articulated. "I wish I had a bit of what you been smoking."

"All right, no need to get shirty; let me give you the example that the Garnishee gave me. Imagine your spaceship as being a needle lying on a rug—you with me so far?"

"The sarcasm we can live without," John huffed. "Get on with it."

"Roger. So, the warpicles reach out and pull on space— the rug now—and pull it toward the needle so that a great big bulge of rug is pulled up in front of the needle. Then the needle is pushed through just two thicknesses of rug, and the bulge is pulled flat, and *zip!* the needle is now a couple of feet away though it only went through two thicknesses of the rug. Simple. You can understand, can't you, Sally?"

"Sure, easy. Do the Garnishee have nice rugs?"

"I hope it works like you say"—John frowned dubiously—"because if it doesn't, we are in for a really rough ride."

"Well, we are just using it as a backup device. We depend upon the cheddite projector for most of the traveling."

"We are here," Slug-Togath announced, coming into the plane with fifty other Garnishee right behind him.

"Who are *we?*" Jerry queried surprisedly.

"Myself and fifty volunteers. I have taken a leave of absence from my work as prime minister and will accompany you with these bravest of the brave. Though every able-bodied Garnishee is needed to rebuild the wreckage of our ruined world, we also have a responsibility to the intelligent life in the universe. You have relieved us of the burden of the Lortonoi and ended the millennia-old war, and we feel that we can do no less for the other races of the galaxy who are oppressed by that bloodthirsty and despicable race of mental leeches."

"Well and nobly said," John concurred.

"Not only that," Slug-Togath continued. "We also hate the bastards with a hatred beyond understanding and would greatly like to be in on the kill when they are smeared, bombed, and destroyed."

"Even better reason." Jerry nodded. "They deserve no mercy. We welcome you and your intrepid followers aboard, please tell them to come well armed and bring plenty of ammo, and it will be a pleasure to fight side by side with them in this just war to save the galaxy."

"Let's drink to that," Sally said smilingly as she came down the aisle pushing the bar cart. "To an alliance for victory. Death to the Lortonoi!"

"Death to the Lortonoi!" they cried with one voice and raised their glasses and downed them. That is, the *humans* drained their glasses. The Garnishee emptied their miniatures of booze into the plastic glasses which they discarded, then ate the bottles since glass acts like an intoxicant with this ancient race.

The engines thundered to life, and the magnificent crusade began.

11

ENCOUNTER IN
DEEP SPACE

Like an arrow hurled from the strongest bow, the refurbished *Pleasantville Eagle* shot into the air, tearing a crackling hole through the atmosphere at twice the speed of sound. The two Earthmen were at the controls while the tentacled, trunklike forms of the Garnishee were at the other stations. Slug-Togath stood behind the pilots where he could coordinate the operation. Sally, very much the hostess in her cheerleader's uniform, was in the aft cabin serving steak sandwiches and drinks to the rows of Garnishee seated there, at the same time complaining bitterly over this menial task. The mighty Garnishee warriors sat unmoving in rapt fascination, listening to the taped jazz program over the headphones at each seat and watching the movie. There was no main feature, but they did not seem to mind, for they took an immense interest in the football training films which they thought were depicting a weird pagan ritual, which perhaps they were.

Once they were on top of the atmosphere and the stars above burned with a cold unflickering light like moth holes in a blanket, Slug-Togath leaned forward and pointed at one of them, a blue point in the eternal darkness.

"There," he said, "is the star to which we have tracked the fleeing Lortonoi spaceship with our omicron radar which detects the action of a space warper. They fled in that direction, but whether they stayed in the vicinity of that star, known to us as Krshtenvlemntu-krm, we do not know."

"Well, we can find out when we get there," said Jerry, adjusting the cheddite projector controls. "And unless I'm wrong, I believe that is the star we call Spica, so let's call it Spica, huh, because it is a lot easier to say."

Since Jerry was the commander, Slug-Togath begrudgingly agreed—but deep down inside he knew it would always be Krshtenvlemntu-krm to him.

"Until we get the bugs worked out of the new cheddite projector, I'm going to take it real easy," Jerry said, adjusting the controls with total absorption. "We'll just jump ahead a teeny bit, maybe just ten light-years and see how we make out."

Everything twitched, and they were ten light-years nearer to Spica, which shone much more brightly now. Corrections were made, and they jumped again. And again. Each time closer, until, after careful and exacting measurements, a final jump was made that would bring them just outside the orbit of the outermost planet that circled this brilliant sun. The jump was made, and instantly every alarm, buzzer, bell, and siren went wild inside the *Pleasantville Eagle*.

They had emerged at the edge of a furious space battle. While Jerry took evasion maneuvers and zipped out of range, the others looked on wide-eyed—and that is a lot of wide eyes since the Garnishee had about twenty-three each—at the fierce engagement that was being played out against the backdrop of stars for their edification. It was an unequal battle, three to one, but the pilot of the single black ship was a master of his craft. No matter how hard they tried, the three pursuing white spacers could not manage to nail the black one which twisted, darted, and dodged with incredible dexterity. Torpedoes flashed out—and missed, while snarling, ravening rays of destruction flicked close—but never close enough to touch the pursued.

"I take my hat off to that pilot," John said with admiration, "he really is a crackerjack."

"But," Jerry inquired, "which side is which?"

"That is a good question," Slug-Togath intoned. "Undoubtedly one side or the other are allies of the Lortonoi who fled this way. Let us contact them on the radio and ask."

This was attempted, but with very little success. There was the hiss and crackle of solar static from the great blue

90

sun and some distant, incomprehensible chatter on the communication bands, nothing else.

"No dice there"—Jerry shrugged—"but I have a better idea. If the Lortonoi are at all involved in that bruhaha out there then there will be some mind reading, mind control, that sort of thing going on because we know they are big for that stuff. So here's what. John, you take the controls. Slug-Togath get behind me and give me a good wrapping with your tentacles, so I can't do any harm. Then take off my mind shield, and I'll try to contact those ships and see who is who so we can come to the aid of the good guys, if there are any. If I get too raunchy or like that, you can put the mind shield back on me and snap me out of it."

"You are a brave man indeed, comrade," Slug-Togath rapped out as he enwrapped Jerry in his unbreakable embrace. "Now prepare yourself, for I remove the mind shield." And he did so, dexterously, with a quick flip of his last tentacle.

"Nothing yet," Jerry said grimly. "I'll just send out a message and see what happens. Hello, warring spaceships, can you read me? I am enemy of the Lortonoi and ready to aid all enemies of those evil-minded leeches. Are any of you there on the same side?"

Suddenly Jerry twitched all over and writhed a bit, then became calm. When he spoke again, it was in a completely different voice, an alien one in fact.

"Very pleased to meet you all, I'm sure. You might say you chaps have come in the old nick of time. Bit of a job keeping these rascals at bay—ooops!—touch of the death ray there bit a chunk out of my tail. If you would like to lend a hand, you could shoot up the three bandits back there who are giving me a hard time."

"Who are you?" John asked.

"Sorry, should have introduced myself. I am Lord Prrsi of the Hagg-Inder, and look, chaps, could we save the rest of the intros for later? There just went one of my stern tubes." They could see the space battle becoming fiercer with every passing instant.

"That's OK," John told him. "But we have to have

something other than your word that you are on our side. We want to contact the three ships that are attacking you."

"Perfectly reasonable request under the circumstances. Look, I'll switch this call to one of the Hagg-Loos in the bandits on my tail. You chat with them and let me know what they say. Over and out."

Instantly a dreadful change came over Jerry. He writhed in the implacable embrace of the Garnishee while his face twisted with incredible fury and from his lips burst a filthy torrent of abuse.

"Tentacled soft-limbed scum of the universe, how dare you invade holy space of Hagg-Loos, filthy democratic republican perverts, we allies of peace-loving Lortonoi will destroy—"

"Enough of that," Slug-Togath said, slapping the mind shield back on Jerry's skull. "Seems pretty obvious."

"Seems even more obvious if you have one of those repulsive creatures stamping through your gray matter," Jerry grated, aligning the cheddite projector in its weapon mode and quickly pressing the activator button three times. On the instant the three enemy spacers vanished and reappeared just above the surface of the burning hot blue sun, and we pretty well know what happened to them then. Jerry took off the mind shield again and instantly spoke in the rounded tones of Lord Prrsi.

"I say, that is a neat way of letting me know what they said to you. Whisk—and they're gone. You must show me that trick. Listen, we ought to have this conversation at closer quarters. That *is* oxygen you're breathing? I thought so, real wizard. Why don't we just match velocity, and I'll join you in your ship. Airlock to airlock, you know the old bit."

As the two voyagers of the space lanes drew close all aboard the *Pleasantville Eagle* could see that Lord Prrsi's ship had not come through the battle unscathed. It was a black dart, almost as long as the 747, but much thinner and without wings. Here and there the skin was seared as though by a blast of heat, and pieces had been bitten out of various parts there and here. Yet the pilot was still smoothly in control and eased up under their wing, and there was only the slightest bump as the newcomer sealed against their newly built airlock. Jerry set the automatic pilot, and they all went back to the cabin to welcome the valiant fighter. There was the hissing of air and a great thumping whumping within the lock, and then, finally, the inner door opened, and the pilot started to come in. Sally screamed and screamed again, and some of the others felt like joining her.

Lord Prrsi, for all his calm and civilized voice when he had spoken through Jerry's body, was a monster. Imagine if you can a twenty-foot-long coal-black chitin-armored, barb-tailed, and claw-rattling scorpion. If you can imagine that, you will have about half an idea of what this alien life form looked like. Not only that, but he was *hot*.

"Rather cold in here," the creature said with a nasal voice. "But I can bear it for a bit. Whom might I have the pleasure?" It turned to face them now, and they realized it had backed into the cabin. Two fiercely glowing red eyes burned down at them from the hideous black head, one of the eyes swollen and distorted by a circular lens the size of a manhole lid that was bolted to supports drilled in the creature's impervious hide. Jerry, no coward he, stepped forward and introduced them all.

"My pleasure," the creature murmured and adjusted the lens before its eye to look at them better.

"You speak pretty good English for a thing that's hot as a brick kiln and looks like a twenty-foot-long black scorpion," John spoke up bravely.

"How *nice* of you to say that," Lord Prrsi said. "If truth be known, I rather pride myself on my linguistic ability; in fact, I led the movement to adopt this new language in place of our old one which was just too clumsy for civilized use. You see we have powerful radio receivers, and we picked up broadcasts from an insignificant little yellow star out in that direction." He waved a great clattering claw. "Oh, I say, I am sorry. Should have realized. It is rather a nice star, for a yellow one, I mean. Since you speak the language, I may assume you come from there? Yes, thought so. Dreadfully rude of me. But I wander. In

93

any case we heard this language emanating from a country named BBC Third Program, and it seemed to fit our needs so we adopted it."

"Could we offer you some refreshment?" Sally asked, ever the perfect little hostess.

"How exceedingly kind of you. I *could* do with a glass of water if it is not too much trouble. I had a drink of water about four months ago, and I'm sure I will be needing more soon so, why not be piggy, have one now, a celebration and all that. Thank you very much, such a *big* one! Enough for five of my people. Well, cheers." He drained the glass in an instant, then wiped his mouth orifice with a clattering, razor-edged claw.

"Could you tell us something about what is happening on your planet and why the fighting and all that?" Jerry asked.

"Indeed I can, and a dreadful story it is. It goes back a *long* time, and if I bore you, please speak up. My race is called the Haggis, and we evolved on the third planet of the sun you see out there. The planet is also called Haggis, which, I suppose, is where our name comes from. In any case the sun is rather bright and hot, and the surface temperature of Haggis is above the boiling point of water over most of the surface, which is one of the reasons why we value this precious fluid so. But I digress. It seems that the incredible burning radiation of the sun produced mutations at a galloping rate, and my people, the Hagg-Inder, developed black chitin to shield us from the sun's rays. But here the race divided, and a subrace, that calls itself the Hagg-Loos in their degenerate tongue, stayed white. Now, aside from the fact that black is beautiful—"

"Keep the faith, baby," John said.

"—it is also good for blocking off radiation. But the white is transparent to the radiation so that the Hagg-Loos had their brains almost cooked out of their sockets after a while. This has produced a race that I can say, without exaggeration, is nuttier than a goober farm. They are insane, evil, degenerate, deprived, depraved, destructful, and desultory. We fought them, but they breed like rabbits in the spring, so in self-defense, we Hagg-Inder emigrated to the

94

fourth planet to get away from them. But they enjoy an evil genius and developed space travel as well, so that a space war has now been going on for over nine thousand years."

"Our war lasted over ten thousand," Slug-Togath said offhandedly.

"How very nice for you," Lord Prrsi intoned cuttingly. "Not to interrupt, but I *was* saying that right bang in the middle of this war the loathsome Lortonoi arrived and were received by the Hagg-Loos with open claws. They really are made for each other, vying for bottom in a loathsomeness contest one might say. They are the only race that has ever willingly joined forces with these interstellar brain leeches. The war intensified then and has been going on at a great rate ever since, and that is about all there is to tell. We trade information with other intelligent, moral, class-ridden societies like our own who fight the Lortonoi, and we can just about hold our own with the new weapons and all that sort of thing. But I talk too much and must be boring you! Please tell me what brings you to our neck of the galaxy, but first, excuse my beastly manners in not mentioning it earlier, but please accept my heartiest thanks for pulling me out of that fix. I bear important messages for our king which I know he will appreciate having."

"Our pleasure," Jerry said. "Our history, in ways, is much like yours. We do come from that yellow sun you mentioned, which we call Sun, and our friends here are from Proxima Centauri back there a ways. We have joined together to do what we can to wipe out the degenerate Lortonoi—"

"Hear! Hear!"

"—and to rescue our friend, Chuck van Chider, who has been captured by them."

"Oh, I say, hard cheese. Captives don't last long with that lot. Even if they mean to hold onto them for a bit, they forget, temptation for a bit of torture creeps up on them until bingo! chap's got no skin or an earful of molten lead, you know the sort of thing. And even if prisoners live for a bit, they turn them over to the Hagg-Loos to

95

work in the incredible DnDrf mines at the North Pole, from out of which no one ever emerges alive."

Sally screamed and fainted.

"We will go after Chuck and rescue him no matter where he is," Jerry said with grim certitude, and all the others nodded agreement, except Sally, who was still unconscious on the floor.

"Well spoken, chaps. Why don't we go back and meet the king and that sort of thing, and perhaps you can tell him about the new weapon, dashed effective I must say, and we'll see what we can find out about your friend?"

Lord Prrsi left then, in somewhat of a hurry since he was beginning to feel the chill, which the others didn't mind since they all were beginning to sweat profusely. The long black ship led the way and signaled ahead so they would not be shot down, and soon they were dropping down toward an immense fortress in the midst of a shell-pocked plane. It was a giant, brooding metal construction that bristled with great gun turrets and detection equipment which tracked their descent. Only at the very last moment did a giant hatch snap open so they could fly in. They did this quickly, as they had been instructed, and the multitonned portal closed on the instant—and just in time —as torpedoes lashed down from space and exploded harmlessly against its invulnerable surface. Lord Prrsi was waiting at the foot of the gangway to meet them when they emerged.

"Welcome to our planet," he said. "I have issued orders that the passageways you will use, as well as the throne room, be lowered in temperature for your convenience. I hope you won't think us rude if we wear these heaters, such as the one hanging from my poison barbed tail."

"Yes, thanks," Jerry said while perspiration burst from his every pore. If this was the "lowered" temperature, he hesitated to think what the heat was normally like in here. Stumbling and sweating, they followed their guide to a great room adorned with stained glass windows and trophies, desiccated white poison barbs undoubtedly from the enemy Hagg-Loos, as well as a dais with a wide golden throne upon it. Upon the throne, wearing a golden crown and a golden space heater on his tail, lay an impressive Hagg-Inder who must be the king.

"May I introduce the king," Lord Prrsi intoned, and they all joined him in bowing low before the majesty upon the throne.

"Oh, I say, do rise, enough of that protocol and poppy-cock. Welcome to our fair planet, and what is this I hear about an invincible weapon you have?" He leaned forward and rubbed two great claws together with a rasping sound.

"It's not exactly a weapon," Jerry explained in detail. "It's really a spaceship drive that can be used as a weapon, like I did with those Hagg-Loos ships. I used the space drive to transport them to the surface of your sun."

"*Utterly* charming, do go on."

"That's about all there is to it. Except we only have the one cheddite projector, and there is a second one, but the Lortonoi stole it and escaped here, and that is why we followed them to try and get it back, and our friend Chuck as well, whom they kidnapped at the same time."

"The Lortonoi have this weapon!" the king gasped and, at the same time, inadvertently closed his claw and snipped in half a six-inch steel bar with which he had been toying. "That could be messy. Lord Prrsi, you know our spy, what's-his-name, charming fellow but of course too pale. Get him on the secret wavelength and find out if he knows anything about all this." Lord Prrsi clacked his claws in salute and scuttled out.

"This spy is a most amusing person," the king said be-musedly as he snipped the steel rod into tiny chunks. "Born an albino, freak of nature and all that, dreadfully hard on his family. But he went to a good school and learned to fight quite well with all the sneers about color and such. Then someone had the delightful idea of surgically implanting an eternium metal case around his brain to shield it from radiation and shipping him off to Haggis as a spy. Worked like a charm. The sodding Hagg-Loos are so insane that anyone with a spark of talent can rise to the top. Our fellow, from a good family and all that, soon rose in the ranks, and now, I do believe, he is the head of their intelligence department or security or something like that. Ahh, my dear Prrsi, that was quick. And your report?"

"Some good news and some bad news, your Highness. First the good. The Lortonoi are in the secret underground laboratory on Haggis and are very annoyed because the Hagg-Loos scientists, mad as hatters all of them, have not yet licked the problem of how to control the cheddite projector. So we won't have to worry about their turning the thing on us for a while. And now the bad news. Your companion, Chuck was the name I believe, would not aid them in their work, and after the usual physical and mental torture they shipped him off to the DnDrf mines, from which there is no return."

"We will save him!" cried Jerry.

"Abandon all hope, it cannot be done."

"I will do it!"

"Well—it *might* be done, but there is only one way. Someone must volunteer to be sold into slavery and be sent to the mine to lead the prisoners in revolt to coincide with an attack from the outside. Any of you chaps want to volunteer for slavery and probably certain death?"

There was a quick shuffling backward by everyone in the room. Slow seconds passed, and guilty looks flashed from under lowered lids. In the end there was one hesitant shuffling footstep after another as Jerry dragged himself reluctantly forward.

"Call up the slavers!" he said, chin up and arms folded staunchly before him. "I volunteer."

A spontaneous cheer ran around the room, and Sally grabbed and kissed him moistly.

12

DISASTER AT THE MINE

"If I'm going through with this scheme I've got to have a lot more info than I have now," Jerry sweated, wiping his forehead with a sweep of his hand. "What is this DnDrf stuff they are mining?"

"Terrible!" Lord Prrsi said, shivering at the thought, and all the other Hagg-Inder quivered as well and, let me tell you, until you have seen a room full of red-hot, quivering, twenty-foot-long black scorpions, you have seen *nothing.* "It is a drug one sniff of which will render the sniffer an addict for life. And an addict will do *anything* to keep the supply coming until, after a few years, the chitin turns to powder and the suffering creature is finally released from the terrible bondage."

"What if you don't have chitin?" John asked, interested.

"What's chitin?" Sally whispered. "I thought it was something you ate."

"That's *chitlin,*" John whispered back. "Chitin is the hard outer covering of most insects and aliens like the Haggis here."

"*Any* time you are through whispering I'll be *happy* to answer your question," Lord Prrsi said, and twitched his great poison sting with annoyance. "The answer is if you don't have chitin, then you are immune to the drug effects of DnDrf. Which is why the cold, soft-fleshed races like yours are sent to the mines. The interstellar slave traders always drop by here knowing they can get a good price for their cargo. And by jingo! there's the answer to your problem of how to get into the mine! Grab the next slave trader that comes along and get sold to him. I would ask for one hundred credits but don't settle for a penny less than eighty-five."

"I do believe a slave trader will be calling in here," the

99

king broke in. "A wonderful idea. And if you could stop the DnDrf trade, we would be ever so grateful."

"If there is a slave trader here," Sally said, putting her pretty little mind to work, "then that means—gasp!—you keep *slaves!*"

"Well, not too many," the king said with a certain amount of guilt oozing out between his words. "We treat them well and that sort of thing, and it does keep the working classes quiet since they miss the worst jobs."

Sally turned her back, folded her arms, sniffed loudly, and said no more. Lord Prrsi was leafing through a sheaf of thin metal sheets marked with strange calligraphy.

"Yes, by Jove!" he elated. "Here's one of the bods just took off this morning. Slow tubs, you know, you can catch him up easily in your ship and flog Jerry to him for a decent price. They'll buy him, then sell him to the Hagg-Loos who will instantly pop him through the one-way door of the DnDrf mine and that is that."

"How will we get out?" Jerry asked.

"That *is* a bit of a problem. Any plans you make with the others will be heard instantly by the mind-reading villains. Of course you could take in a batch of miniaturized mind shields; we have some nice ones."

They were indeed nice, no bigger than the head of a pin. Yet when one of them was breathed up a nostril and lodged in a sinus cavity it would go instantly to work, activated by the moisture and the warmth, and provide as good a mind shield as the bulky caps supplied by the Garnishee. A supply was provided and woven into Jerry's jockstrap, the theory being that if they took away his clothes and shoes, they would at least leave him *that*. The Hagg-Loos may have been insane monsters, but they wouldn't go that far. Then Jerry's clothes were torn and whip marks painted on his skin, and they all returned to the delicious cool of the *Pleasantville Eagle* and shot off after the slavers.

It was only a matter of minutes before they caught up with them in their parabola course that took their ship well outside the battle zone. John pulled up alongside the rusty, streaked, stained, filthy vessel and called them on the radio.

"Hello, slave ship, do you read me?"

"We prefer to be called Employment Counselors," came the whining answer in reply.

"We have an employee here maybe we can bring to you for counseling."

"A slave for sale?" came the slobbering answer. "State the specifications."

"Male, strong, stupid, loves obeying orders, low-temperature life form suitable for the DnDrf mines. I want a hundred credits for it."

"You'll take eighty-five or you'll take nothing."

"Eighty-five it is. Match airlocks and we'll pass him over. See that the money is passed back in its place."

"We are honest businessmen performing a vital function in society and would never consider cheating on a legitimate transaction of this kind. Besides, we see your gun turrets."

Shoulders back, back straight, Jerry walked into the airlock and heard the heavy inner door close behind him like the sealing of a vault. The outer door opened into the slaver's airlock, where an ugly creature at least seven feet tall was waiting for him. It was humanoid but repulsive and carried a whip, which it instantly put to work driving Jerry before it, tossing a sack of credits back over its shoulder as it left. Jerry moved along quickly enough under this impetus and soon after found himself chained to a bar in the metal wall between two other slaves. They looked at him apathetically as is the slave's wont, but he took a greater interest in them.

"How do you do," he said to the slave on his right, a creature who was very humanoid, though bright red even to the eyeballs, and who had what might be called a normal left hand—if seven fingers are normal—but instead of a right hand the arm had a bony sword from the elbow down. This sword looked hard and efficient and rather sharp so that when the creature only answered with a guttural snarl and a jab at Jerry with the sword, he adroitly dodged aside and caught the red jaw of the other cleanly with his fist and laid him out for the count.

"Very neatly done," a deep voice resounded from beside him. "One should never waste time talking with the red swordsmen of Vindaloo. They have tiny minds and only know fighting, whereas my people of Bachtria are civilized and intelligent. May I introduce myself—I am called Pipa Pipa, but you may call me Pipa if that pleases you."

The individual who spoke was chained to Jerry's left. A fat, green, dampish sort of alien with a great white belly. His eyes protruded from his head, and his mouth slashed across the entire width of his great head. He must have come from a water world because his knobby fingers were connected by webs.

"My pleasure," Jerry said. "My name is Jerry Courteney."

"Then I may call you Courteney?"

"Jerry would be better."

"I understand," Pipa croaked. "Hist, the overseer comes, we must not be seen talking or it means the lash." He sighed deeply. "Not that it matters. *Everything* means the lash."

He sighed again as the whip fell across his back, and the overseer went down the line lashing right and left.

"On your feet, you scum of the universe," he bawled hoarsely with rough glee. "We have arrived at your new home. You'll love it here. The DnDrf mines of Haggis!"

A sound, something between a moan and a groan, emanated from the filthy ranks, for this was known as the end of the road for slaves, from which none ever returned. With reluctance they rattled their chains as they were unlocked and driven toward the door.

"This is the end!" Pipa groaned. "I shall never see my home pond again."

Jerry wanted to give him some measure of cheer, but he dared not, not yet. The mind shield in his sinus prevented his brain being read like an open book, but he knew that all the others could have their thoughts tapped at any

102

time. He must keep his secret safe! The time would come. . . .

Whips cracking like lightning, the slavers drove the hapless slaves down the gangway and into the frigid Artic wastes of Haggis. Of course, they were frigid by Haggisian standards, which meant the temperature was around 100 degrees by Fahrenheit standards, which is bearable, though not very comfortable. As each slave emerged, the slavers stripped him and-or her of all their clothing so they could survive in the dry heat. Jerry's Hush Puppies were cut from his feet with the slash of a blade, and his sundered tie-died Levi's followed them. All that remained was his jockstrap, and he was ready to fight to the death to keep this——and not *only* for the mini-mind shields—but because it was bright purple, the slavers thought it was part of his body (which shows you how slavers think) and they pushed him on with the others. Ahead were the mines.

It was a scene of utter desolation. All about lay a sulfur desert, cooking and shimmering in the heated air. Above hung the great blue sun of Sirius, frying brains in their brain-pans and shooting out hard radiation to batter genes and start the mutations mutating. Ahead lay a mountain range, and set into the nearest mountain was a solid collapsium door just six feet high.* Above this door was engraved in letters carved out of the solid rock "Abandon Hope All Ye Who Enter Here" or something like that. Jerry could not be sure because he could not read Haggisian, but it seemed a reasonable guess. The whips cracked even more fiercely as they drove the reluctant slaves toward this grim portal.

"Now hear this," the master slaver bellowed through a loudhailer from a position on a rock where he could survey the gathered, trembling, fear-infested slaves, who were quickly whip-cracked into silence.

"I'm only gonna tell this to you just once, so cock your

* Collapsium is an artificial material made of atoms with their binding energy reduced so they sort of collapse in upon themselves and are dense and heavy and that kind of thing.

ears and bend your antenna or whatever. This here is the mine I been telling you about. That door there is the first of seventeen just like it. The drill is that it opens, one of you slobs goes in, then it closes before the next door opens. You go through that etc. etc. until you are in the mine. It is my poisonal suggestion that you step lively because three seconds after a door opens a fifty-six-thousand-volt current is sent through the compartment you will be standing in. So in you go, crying and weeping, but in you go. Once inside, you will find more slaves working away at mining the DnDrf. The Hagg-Loos don't bother about how the stuff is mined, and they don't care neither. Grinding machines inside grind it to a fine powder, and it is pumped out through a one-inch pipe. One ton of it a day. As long as that ton comes out every day, food and water are pumped in through other pipes. No workee, no eatee, as the expression goes. So do your best, work for your chow, resign yourself to a last look at the sun for eternity, and off you go into endless darkness."

The whips cracked again as the outer door opened, and the first slave was booted into position. One by one the others followed until it was Jerry's turn, and he took a last despairing look at the burning plain, the slaver ship, the insulated buildings where the Hagg-Loos were; then in he went. With an unoiled screeching the portal closed behind him, and darkness descended.

"I'm doing it for you, Chuck," he said staunchly, then sniffed and wiped his nose with the back of his hand. When the next door opened, he skittered through quickly as he heard the onrushing 56,000 volts zinging through the cables toward him.

It was a nightmare voyage with an even more nightmarish ending. As Jerry stepped through the last door, a great, hairy, ugly, brutal monster of a slave caught him in the back of the neck with a club (that looked suspiciously like a human femur), sending him sprawling. But surprised as he had been by the sudden and unprovoked attack, Jerry's reflexes were still superb, and he rolled with the blow so it did not stun him, fell and twisted and caught the brute's shin with a solid kick that knocked him to the ground.

Then, before the foul creature could recover, he dived on it and clutched hard with a Japanese headlock that renders the victim unconscious in five seconds and dead in ten. He applied full pressure. The thing tried to speak through its filthy beard. At the end of four seconds it gasped, "Urgh . . . Jerry . . . don't . . ." and instantly became limply unconscious on the fifth second. Jerry thought about this for a few seconds more, wondering how the creature knew his name. After eight seconds had passed, he looked at it more closely, and at the end of nine seconds he released the pressure so that blood reentered the thing's brain, and it did not die. Its grimy, bloodshot eyes opened tremblingly, and it glared up with bestial hatred.

"Chuck, that *is* you, isn't it?" Jerry asked.

The thing blinked fuzzily and muttered, "Me name Chuck . . . how you know name?"

"Poor lad," Jerry said, helping him to his feet and dusting him off. "They have been walking through his brain with spiked boots, and they shall pay for it, and someday, I promise, he will be restored to full mental and physical health. Do you understand, Chuck?"

"Let's go eat. Chuckee hungry."

Jerry patted the Chuck-thing on the shoulder and led him toward the chow trough, where the others were guzzling, concealing his deepest feelings at this terrible fate that had struck his best friend. He felt no desire to compete with the others for the thin gruel that they lapped up by the handfuls. It looked and smelt like mashed mangel-wurzels. In fact, it probably was mashed mangel-wurzels; these fiends would stop at nothing. So, while Chuck dived into the swill, Jerry looked around at the demoniac scene —and that was a good word for it, for the cave was dimly lit by flickering flames that leaped from niches scraped in the stone walls. These fires were fueled with some sort of dark lumps; he noticed this when one of the slaves dragged over a bucket and dumped some of them on a fire. A loud creaking and groaning filled the air as other slaves worked hard at the great handles of a grinding machine. This was fed with chunks of some black substance wheeled up on carts. The mill reduced it to a fine powder which was dumped into a funnel and vanished down a pipe.

"DnDrf!" he gasped aloud, the terrible drug that drove aliens mad, then ate away their chitin. Reluctantly he sidled up for a closer look and kicked at a glistening chunk that had dropped from the mill.

"You know," he mused to himself. "If I did not know that this was the hideous drug called DnDrf, I would say it is nothing but a lump of coal."

"It *is* only a lump of coal, for DnDrf is coal," a grating voice said from behind him. "You think you are a smart guy, huh!"

Jerry was beginning to catch onto the interpersonal relationships in the mine, so he ducked and dodged before turning so that the club, a human femur with a stone head, whistled by without hitting him.

"Try that again and you are a dead thing," he said to the thing wielding the club, crouching at the same time in the karate instant-death-mode.

The creature stopped and looked at him bemusedly, and he looked at it. It wasn't much to look at. Humanoid in form and about his height, it was covered with lumpy brown hide that had a crumbly texture. Only its eyes gleaming whitely from its misshapen head.

"I am called Fevil Dood," it grunted. "And I am top slave in this compound. Do you want to challenge me? Means fight to the death."

"Quite the opposite," Jerry simpered in a sucking way. A plan was already beginning to form. "I will obey all your commands and am completely at your disposal. Just tell me the drill here and show me where I fit in."

"Unghh," the thing grunted, reluctantly lowering its weapon. "Better be telling the truth, or you die like quick. Me and my boys run this place and do no work other than bash skulls in. You and other slaves dig the DnDrf, crush it, and pump it out, a ton a day. You do this every day, and we let you eat and drink and live."

"What do you get out of it?"

"We eat and drink and live; only we don't work."

106

"Seems a dull existence. I should think you would be planning ways to crack out of here."

"Forget it. You here to stay. We all thought about it; now we don't think about it any more. So work."

"Sure. But why did those two guys stop working?"

"Where?" Fevil Dood roared, raising the club and spinning about.

Jerry instantly gave him a chop on the neck that dropped him, unconscious, with a thud, to the ground. Working fast, Jerry plucked one of the mind shields from its hiding place and then sat on the alien's rough brown chest. With one hand he held Fevil's mouth shut, and with the other he pinched shut his nostrils. Even though unconscious, Fevil began to feel short of breath and groaned and writhed. When his skin was turning purple under the brown, Jerry relented and opened one nostril. As the torrent of air was sucked into his nose Jerry dropped the mind shield into the slipstream, and it vanished into the recesses of the creature's head. At this moment Fevil arched his back and sent Jerry spinning away. Seizing his club, he roared and attacked.

"Now just one moment," Jerry explained, dodging the blows. "If you will please stop that for a moment, I'll tell you what's going on."

The angry boss slave was not interested in explanations, though, and roared and chased Jerry about the cave, cheered on by the other slaves, who were glad of this bit of entertainment plumped into their monotonous existence. Jerry was getting tired of this, so the next time he ducked a blow he plucked up a lump of coal—and suddenly whirled about. The athlete who had batted .999 consistently and had pitched forty-two no-hit games in a row could hit the target he aimed at, oh, indeed he could! The coal whistled through the air and clunked off Fevil Dood's forehead and laid him low one more time. Jerry seized up the club and chased the other slaves away, then sat and waited, club raised, for the defeated superslave to recover. Recover he did, within moments, and glared up at the raised club.

"So go ahead and kill me already. See how you like being boss of these dumbheads."

"*Shut up!*" Jerry hissed. "Listen quietly or I will brain you. I knocked you out so I could insert a mind shield in your nose. I am here to lead an escape from this mine."

Fevil Dood's eyes popped out three inches, on stalks, at this news. "You know, you're right," he mused. "I am a simple telepath but realize now I am getting no messages. So that means no one can listen in on my brain either?"

"Dead right. Now if I give you the club back, will you help me organize the slaves for a revolt?"

"I'm your alien!" he bellowed, leaping to his feet. "Let's go!"

They went. One by one his gang of bullyboys and over-muscled slobs was called aside and bashed on the head so a mind shield could be inserted. Once consciousness was recovered and the plan explained, the recruit instantly aided the head banging of the others. This went on until all the mind shields had been dispensed to the waiting sinuses, and the gang of eager thugs gathered around.

"Gather around," Jerry ordered, "and I will explain the escape plan. Our part will be to—"

"AHHHHHHHHHH!" Fevil Dood said loudly. Jerry glared at him.

"Will you kindly shut the hell up?" he hinted.

"AHHHHHHHHHH!" was his only answer. He went on, trying to ignore the interruption.

"As I was saying, our job is to overpower the guards outside."

"But," a great thug covered with tarnished scales asked, "how do we get out?"

"That will be done by—"

"AHHHHHHHH—CHOOOOO!" Fevil Dood exploded, sneezing with great force. With such great force indeed that his mind shield was expelled from his hairy nostril and shot across the cave to vanish in the darkness.

"*Gesundheit,*" Jerry said, politely.

"What is this meeting?" Fevil Dood asked in clipped, suspicious tones. "What are you all doing together? Why

108

cannot I enter your minds? Aha, I see it all in the dim mind of this stupid creature! You are planning escape!"

Thunk the club said as it contacted the side of Fevil Dood's now rather bashed-up skull.

"He lost his mind shield," Jerry explained, "and a Hagg-Loos took over his mind. Now that they know we must push on with the plan!"

"You're not just gnashing your fangs," a slave said, rather well endowed himself with fangs. "Take a look at the rest of the mob!"

Every slave in the immense cave, other than those in this brave little band, had now ceased work and turned in their direction. Zombielike they raised their hands and clawed their fingers, their eyes blazed with alien fury as, with a shambling, hideous motion they advanced.

"They've been taken over by the guards," Jerry shouted. "Fall back this way, men. I'm sending out the message to start the attack."

He bit down hard in a certain way upon a certain tooth.

"Ow!" he screeched. "I've gone and broken a damn filling. Wrong tooth."

Now, biting down in a certain way upon the *right* tooth, he actuated an incredibly tiny, yet exceedingly powerful subetheric radio which sent out a prerecorded signal. Out the signal blasted through the seams of coal and the solid stone, out across the searing plain and into space and through the mountain range behind which the waiting *Pleasantville Eagle* was waiting.

He hoped. "Fight men, fight, for the signal has gone out and help is on the way."

It was an unequal battle, because for every slave bopped on the head and knocked out, two more sprang forward to take his place. And the slaves were ruthless, just slaves to their possessors' slightest whim, not caring if they were maimed or killed. On and on they came, and the defenders retreated step by step until their backs were to the stone wall and their numbers greatly diminished. Then, when all appeared to be lost, something incredible happened. A glare of light blasted forth, and they all

109

stopped and gaped. Well, it wasn't really much of a glare, in fact, it was kind of dim, but their eyes were so used to the eternal darkness that it *looked* like a glare to them. For, in a single microscopic instant of time, all the indestructible series of one-way doors had vanished and in their place was a smooth-walled tunnel leading to the outside. The cheddite projector had whisked away all the portals and part of the surrounding rock so that the way to liberty was open.

"The way to liberty is open!" Jerry roared. "Follow me!"

His gang of club-wielding rowdies roared in answer and galloped through the other slaves who were now milling about disturbedly, some still under brain control, others released from this vile bondage. Down the tunnel Jerry ran, waving the club, fleet-footed and fast—one stumble and he would have been trampled to a pulp—and out onto the plain to engage the emerging guards in battle. Behind them in the cave the other slaves found themselves free of control and also headed for liberty.

Although the Hagg-Loos fought like the mad devils that they were, they never stood a chance. For not only did they have to face their enraged slaves, but from the plane burst John and a squad of Garnishee, as well as five Hagg-Inder warriors, led by Lord Prrsi, who charged out of the cargo hold. The battle was short, sweet, and bloody, and soon nothing but fragments of steaming Hagg-Loos flesh littered the landscape and the last defender was dead.

"Into the plane!" Lord Prrsi ordered. "Reinforcements are on the way, and I don't think we are up to facing their entire battle fleet."

"Hold on!" Jerry called out, battling his way against the stream of slaves pouring into the 747. "Where's Chuck? After all, we *did* come here to release him; that was the idea of the whole thing."

"He's not in the plane or in this bunch," John mused.

"Then he's still in the cave," Jerry called out and ran that way in the instant.

"Come back!" Lord Prrsi ordered. "We cannot wait, for if we do so, we risk the loss of the cheddite projector, as

110

well as all aboard your ship, not to mention the ship itself."

"You just stay there and wait for me," Jerry commanded. "I'll only be a moment. Fight if you must, but just hold on a bit."

Then he was pounding into the cave once more and, frankly, getting sort of pooped and out of breath after the recent bout of activity. Inside the cave he could see nothing, since his eyes were now adjusted to the glare outside. "Chuck!" he called, and "Chuck!" again, but there was no answer. Stumbling blindly along, he made his way to the food troughs—had he heard a slurping noise?—and there, sure enough, was his buddy, head down in the gruel and slurping away.

"We have to get out of here!" He pulled at Chuck's resisting shoulder.

"Booger off!" was the growled answer. "Chuck eet him food."

Jerry's arm was sore when he raised it, and the edge of his hand hurt when he administered the karate chop to the muscular neck below him. It was a job to get the dead weight of his friend onto his shoulder, but he did manage, then staggered out of the tunnel once again. A steak and a hot bath was what he needed after this, he thought to himself, and maybe a couple of good belts of bourbon.

Then the entrance was ahead, and he staggered and stumbled and stopped. High above he could see the diving forms of Hagg-Loos fighters, weapons glistening and ready.

But, before him on the battle-scarred plain where the *Pleasantville Eagle* had stood there was nothing. Absolutely nothing.

They were alone, trapped on this enemy planet so far from home.

What a hideous way to die. . . .

13

TRAPPED ON HAGGIS

It was a moment of ghastly paralysis for this intrepid space explorer, who, at this instant, was beginning to regret very much the whole idea of space exploration. What to do? Suicide seemed about the only answer, and he let the unconscious Chuck slip heavily to the ground while he considered possible means of terminating a life that was just about as good as terminated anyway. The moment passed, and he abandoned thoughts of suicide for the moment, mainly because he could not see any easy way of doing it, short of drowning himself in the mashed mangel-wurzels which didn't sound attractive at all. Above him the Hagg-Loos fighting ships raced and cavorted and occasionally banged off their guns at suspicious objects on the ground below, but other than the cooked lumps of slain Haggisians and an occasional slave corpse or two, the landscape was empty.

Or was it? What was that strange sort of rattling, slithering sound that came from behind the heaped-up rocks? Reflexively, Jerry withdrew into the tunnel mouth, pulling Chuck after him. The scraping grew louder and louder until, with horrifying abruptness, the great pallid form of a Hagg-Loos appeared. Its poison barb twitched, its faceted, evil eyes stared at the tunnel—and then it attacked!

Fast as it was, Jerry was just as fast. With Chuck in tow he sprinted into the mine and dived for the grinding machine.

"Enter at your own peril!" he shouted, raising a handful of the deadly coal dust, coal dust to him, but drug-addicting DnDrf to the Hagg-Loos who now clattered into the cave after him.

"You heard me," Jerry cried, backing away. "I mean it.

One step more and I let fly and you are an addict for life until your chitin rots away!"

But the Hagg-Loos warrior ignored him and still came forward. Good as his word, Jerry let fly unerringly with the coal dust, which shmeared itself on the enemy's white chitin. And still it came. Jerry abandoned the coal-dust ploy and seized up one of the clubs, not much of a weapon against the yard-long nippers of the enemy, but if fight he must, why, then he would die fighting.

"To me, Chuck, to me!" he called out. "I may have to die fighting, and a little help would be appreciated."

But the help was not coming. Chuck had regained consciousness and was back at the mangel-wurzel trough, noshing away with bestial slurping sounds. The enemy advanced until its great form hovered over Jerry, and he drew back his club for one last blow when a trapdoor opened in its abdomen and a mop of tentacles popped out.

"I know those familiar tentacles," Jerry exulted, hurling the club aside. "That is you, isn't it, Slug-Togath?"

"None other," came the gloomy answer. "Left behind by force despite strong reservations as to wisdom of abandonment, to aid in effecting your escape."

"Damn good idea on someone's part. Am I allowed to ask just what you are doing inside one of the enemy?"

"Not enemy, giant robot machine constructed after you were sold to the slavers. It seems that the Hagg-Inder albino spy on this planet was interrupted during a secret message, and they have not been able to contact him yet. So this robot was built, and I agreed to take it into the enemy city to see about the spy, but under controlled conditions and etc., not just dumped at the North Pole like this." His tentacles wriggled with self-pity as he gave his TS card a good verbal punching.

"Cheer up, old Medusa head," Jerry chirruped, patting him on the back, inadvertently giving him a black eye at the same time since, of course, he had eyes on his back as well. "You've got help on this mission now, one and one-eighth good men to help you. Chuck being the one-eighth, about all he is good for since they crunched his brain." Chuck happily slurped an answer.

113

"Look, tell me about it later, will you?" Slug-Togath said nervously, peering in all directions, which of course was easy for him to do. "Climb into this damn thing so I can seal the hatch before any of them spots us."

And this they did, only getting Chuck away from the mangel-wurzels with some difficulty and by promising him an Ormoloo-burger if he was a good boy and climbed into the Haggis machine and sat quietly. This was done and the hatch slammed, and Jerry looked around approvingly at the well-organized, though cramped, quarters. A control seat in the head with vision screens to operate the machine, with special controls for the poison sting in the tail which also housed a supersonic crumbler beam. Tool and food compartments were on both sides, a compact galley, recruiting posters and VD warnings on the walls, a folding cot, a color TV next to the bar, and a chemical toilet tucked discreetly in the rear behind a curtain. "Not bad, not bad at all," Jerry approved as he sizzled up a burger for the salivating Chuck, who was strapped into a chair. It smelled so good he made one himself and was munching away under the disapproving eyes of Slug-Togath.

"I know your Earthling axiom about Nero fiddling while Rome burned," he disapproved, "and we have the equivalent in our axiom about how only a *crogis nardles* while his friend's mother *cakarakas.*"

"Sounds sort of dirty," Jerry mumbled around a mouthful, "so don't bother to translate. While eating I have been thinking, and I have a plan of escape, but first I've got a couple of questions. Like do you have a mind shield for Chuck, since the enemy might think something was wrong if they caught his brutish thoughts emanating from the neighborhood of this thing's big intestine?"

"Not to worry. The entire device is mind-shielded. They will catch no stray thoughts."

"That's a good beginning. But what about if they should try to contact what they think is their buddy here and get no thoughts in return?"

"I assure you, all this was taken into consideration when the device was constructed. There is a programmed brainwave transmitter hooked to the antenna. This is the

114

board that controls it. By selecting the correct button, it will broadcast thoughts of immense concentration, including the message 'buzz off and don't bug me now,' the random thoughts of deep sleep, and so forth."

"What is this button labeled 'section 8'?"

"Well, as I am sure you know, all the Hagg-Loos are insane to a greater or lesser degree, usually greater, driven that way by the maddening hard radiation of their sun, the great star Spica. Many of the creatures have periods of frothing insanity at which time the others leave them completely alone. That is the frothing insanity button."

"Then that is *all* I need to know!" Jerry shouted and did a little victory dance. "My plan is now complete. Prepare to escape."

As soon as the plan had been explained to him, the dubious Slug-Togath became an enthusiast as well and joined in the preparations. Using the great front claws, they dug into the powdered coal dust and hurled it all over the white body of the machine. Then, with all claws full of more coal dust, they raced for the entrance, and before they emerged, Jerry pressed the section 8 button.

Oh, what a hideous sight it was to the Hagg-Loos warriors who were emerging from the fighting ships. For, in their institutional madness, they fear nothing in the universe other than the dread DnDrf which would bring on addiction, rotted chitin, you know the drill. So they took one glimpse at what appeared to be one of their number just *coated* with the deadly substance, stoned out of his mind obviously and radiating nuttiness on every wavelength, and coming in *their direction*.

They split. Those still in their ships blasted off instantly. Those near their ships dived into them, in many cases slamming the doors in their comrades' faces. These, and the others too far from the ships, instantly fled at top speed into the frigid 110 degree Artic wastes.

It worked like a charm. Slug-Togath labored at the controls, his tentacles a blur of motion as he spun the machine about and headed for the grounded spaceships, their owners fleeing before him. Still mentally broadcasting crazy like crazy, he clambered the machine into the first

one with an open port, slamming and sealing the port behind. The control cabin was in the nose, and in a matter of
seconds he and Jerry examined and figured out how they
worked, and *whammo!* the ship blasted free from the
ground and rose erratically into the air. Moments later
they were alone, arcing up into space in a high parabola.

"What's next?" Jerry asked pouring himself a large
martini cocktail and draining it almost instantly.

"Food for Chuckee," that pathetic voice entreated, so
Jerry went and fried up another batch of Ormoloo-
burgers.

"They'll try to intercept us and blast us out of space, so
we are getting out of space before they can report and locate us. This orbit will bring us down a few miles outside
Haggis City, where we will abandon the ship and proceed
to the rendezvous with the Hagg-Inder spy, or at least to
the place where he is supposed to be, to determine the nature of the trouble."

Night arrived suddenly as they caught up with the planet's rotation, and darkness concealed their fall.

"Controls are set," Slug-Togath reported. "When this
ship lands, we have just four seconds to get out of it before it takes off on a random course that I have
programmed into the computer. I am sure that they will
disintegrate the ship so that all the DnDrf in it will be destroyed. As long as we are not seen emerging we will be
safe."

With these words barely out of his mouth, Slug-Togath
dived the ship behind a screening row of hills and into a
shallow valley. The instant they touched the door sprang
open, and the machine, under his deft control, sprang
through it—and just in time, for the closing portal actually
brushed the poison sting of the immense form. Whooshing
and roaring, the ship took off and, no more than a few
seconds later, a flight of fighting rockets rushed by over-
head, following it, the first light of dawn painting their
white forms a bright blue.

"There is one thing you have to do before we leave
here," Jerry said, filling a plastic bucket with water at the
116

sink. "Take this and a scrubbing brush and get out there and remove every particle of coal dust so this thing is pristine and clean again."

"Whaddaya mean *I* have to do?" protested Slug-Togath. "I'm a prime minister at home and I'm not used to that kind of menial labor."

"Agreed, but you also have a hide so tough it bounces off bullets, which is more than I can say for my all too tender flesh. This machine is air-conditioned, but the thermometer tells me that it is a cozy two hundred and fifty degrees outside, which would fry me instantly. On your way, old Medusa, consider yourself a volunteer!"

Grumbling, the Garnishee slipped through the door, admitting a wave of roasting heat, and began a clean scrubdown fore and aft. Jerry had another belt at the gin and then closed his eyes for a quick and well-deserved nap. Chuck, stomach full at last, dozed as well, and it was real neat until another blast of heat announced Slug-Togath's return.

"Pfffft," he said, and dust came out of his mouth when he spoke. His hide was wrinkled, and he was only about half as thick as he had been when he went out. Jerry looked on with interest as the Garnishee hooked a plastic hose to the faucet on the sink, then stuck it into one of the orifices in his body and turned the water on. He began to swell slowly and to lose the desiccated look.

"Little hot out there?" Jerry asked innocently, and smiled at the glare shot back at him from about a dozen bloodshot eyes. "As soon as you fill your tank, we'll get on with the job. Did you say what was the name of the secret agent we had to contact?"

"I didn't say," Slug-Togath burbled with hydratory relief. "It is a secret."

"Well not from me, for chrissake," Jerry said petulantly. "Give."

"Operator X-9," Slug-Togath whispered. "Better to commit suicide than to give that name away."

"I'll remember, I'll remember. What next?"

"We go to Haggis City. As we were landing, I noticed a

117

monorail line not too far from here. Perhaps we can obtain transportation that way and not drain the batteries on this machine."

"Sounds good—lead the way."

Bluey-fingered dawn had brightened the landscape as they climbed out of the rift and looked down at the plain. Sure enough the towers of a monorail line cut close by, and they could see a station not too far distant. They hurried the machine in that direction and only slowed when they saw other Hagg-Loos ahead. More and more appeared, crawling out from under rocks where they lived, waving good-bye to their mates, giving their young cheerful nips on the chitin with their claws as they departed.

"It looks like we hit the rush hour," Jerry mused. "All the commuters going to work in the morning. Do you have a broadcast mental program for this?"

"I should think so . . . here, how about this one. *Memories of an Orgy,* a program designed to be eavesdropped on but not interrupted."

"Say, I'd like to hear that one myself! Though on second thought maybe I wouldn't. All those claws, crackling chitin, waving antennae. No, let them enjoy it."

Strolling casually, they joined the Hagg-Loos, who were moving along the rock pathways and converging on the station. More than one antenna dipped and trembled in their direction—that recording must have been a doozy!—but they were not bothered. Clambering up the stairs, they had only a short wait before the shining cars of the monorail train whooshed into the station. There was a rush for seats, and of course the experienced commuters got there first and snapped open the metallic sheets of their morning newsfax and hid behind them. The ride was not a long one, and before they knew it, the train had stopped at the immense Padng-tun station in Haggis City and the commuters rushed for the exits. Slug-Togath made sure that they went slower than the others, then pointed out why.

"See—as each one approaches the exit, it produces a pass of some kind which it shows to the officer stationed there."

118

"We have no pass?" Jerry queried.

"You took the words right out of my speaking hole."

"Then let's try in the opposite direction, back along the track. There will be freight exits, workers' entrances, something. And they will be a little more deserted if there is any trouble."

Clattering along casually on its twenty claw-tipped feet, the hulking form of the Hagg-Loos robot trotted away from the rushing workers. The platform ended in a metal gate with an unreadable inscription, and after a quick look around, Jerry cut the gate in half with a quick snick of the claws. There was a ramp beyond that plunged into the bowels of the station, so into the bowels they plunged.

"Don't you think we should change the porno broadcast to something more suitable for the occasion?" Jerry asked.

"Sound idea. There is a program here of the mental retardation of a longtime DnDrf sniffer whose chitin is about to go soft."

"No, I think not, not in a railroad station."

"Then how about this. A low-type mind working on computations for betting on the daily *jeddak* races."

"That's more like it, sort of person who would work here, I imagine. Plug it in."

They entered an area of wide corridors and great stacks of boxes. Occasionally a flatbed cargo carrier would appear, driven by a Hagg-Loos, but they were so noisy that they announced their arrival, and there was always time to hide. Soon after this they found one of the cargo carriers standing idle, and after a swift look at the controls, they climbed their machine aboard. With a twist of the handles they were off, moving much faster now, part of the busy workings and ignored by all the other workers they passed. Jerry was whistling happily when they spotted a high arched exit ahead with a patch of blue sky shining through.

"This looks like it," he told Slug-Togath. "Press the button, and let's get out of here."

They rumbled forward and were almost free of the station when the ugly form of a Hagg-Loos popped out of an opening in the wall. A very official-looking monster

119

with *cop* written all over it, from the golden shield nailed to its chitin in front to the ugly-looking weapon it clutched, and even to the flat claws on its feet. As the thing trundled in their direction, Jerry flipped a switch that allowed thoughts to enter but not leave.

"You *jeddak* racing fan moron," the thought arrived, "what do you think you are doing driving out of the station with that load of bombs? Can't you read? Now let me see your ID, and get away from those controls before I let you have it."

It was disaster.

14
BIRTH OF THE
GALAXY RANGERS!

Really a disaster for the cop. Jerry was ready at the gun controls, and he swiveled the tail about and pressed the right button, and from the poison sting the supersonic crumbler beam lashed out. The hapless minion of the law instantly crumbled into a heap of white chitin dust, and the cargo carrier rumbled on.

But the alarm was out! Sirens warbled and alarms clanged while the guards converged from all directions.

"We had better leave the cargo carrier here," Slug-Togath shouted, busy at the controls.

"Not just leave it—make them a real present of it!" Jerry yodeled, spinning the wheel that sent the clumsy machine crashing into the doorway.

Great motors hummed in the legs of their robot Hagg-Loos machine as it jumped clear just in time. At full power they sprinted away from the station and the growing excitement at the jammed exit, and just before they turned the corner, Jerry sighted carefully and put a quick zap of the heat ray into the load of bombs.

They blew up nicely indeed, shaking the ground with a mighty thunder and bringing down half the station behind them. Chortling, they fled, strolled rather, so they would not be noticed. Inside the strolling machine Slug-Togath unfolded a map of Haggis City that the spy had sent them and guided them swiftly toward the secret lair of the spy, X-9.

"Careful now," Jerry cozened, "we are getting close."

"I can read a map just as well as you can," Slug-Togath grumbled.

"That's nice," Jerry mused. "Say, do you notice that that manhole lid—the one over there about twelve feet in diameter—is sort of lifted up, and I think I can see two glowing eyes watching us from under it."

"The police!" Slug-Togath wailed, and his tentacles stumbled over the controls so that their robot danced a little two-step on the pavement.

"Easy does it there, old squid-head," Jerry consoled. "Don't get carried away until we find out what it is. Might just be the sewer men at work, you know."

From a loudspeaker on the wall came an impatient hissing.

"The manhole is also hissing," Jerry observed. "And it may just be hissing for attention. Let's sidle over in that direction."

Attempting to look innocent, the twenty-foot-long machine disguised as a great white scorpion foxtrotted sideways until it was close to the manhole. The glowing eyes followed them, and when they were close a hoarse voice whispered, "One, two, three, four, five. . . ."

"The password!" Slug-Togath shouted, then switched on an external loudspeaker. "Six, seven, eight, nine, ten," he said into it.

"What kind of cockamamie password is that?" Jerry asked, aggrieved. "A five-year-old could figure that one out."

"It's what they call native psychology." The manhole lifted higher, and a white claw beckoned them forward. After a quick look around to make sure they weren't being watched, the machine shot forward and down the giant manhole. "The Hagg-Loos have such short tempers that they can't count past four without getting so irritated they stop. In this manner do we know that the great beast lurking here is none other than the Hagg-Inder spy who goes by the name of X-9."

"Hiya, X-9," Jerry said into the microphone.

"You took your own sweet time about getting here," X-9 grumbled. "I been lurking in this damn sewer so long that I'm covered with fungus."

"Hazard of the game," Jerry said offhandedly, ignoring the other's bitter tongue. "We came as soon as we could after you stopped answering the radio on the secret wavelength. What happened?"

"They caught me cracking into the secret laboratory and became suspicious. I talked them out of it for a while; after all, I *am* head of intelligence on this filthy planet. But I couldn't convince the Lortonoi of my innocence, they were too shrewd for that, and when they wanted to subject me to their infamous mind-vacuum technique, I fled and have been hiding out here ever since waiting for you."

"But you know the location of the secret laboratory!" Slug-Togath exulted.

"That I do."

"Would someone let me in onto what's going on?" Jerry muttered petulantly.

"Chuckee hungry," a new voice said as Chuck woke up with a wide yawn.

"Here is what has happened since you were sold into slavery," Slug-Togath explained, counting off the different points on his tentacle tips. "First, experiments showed that the new cheddite was far stronger than the original piece, perhaps owing to the presence of certain gastric acids of your female companion. More experiments are planned to determine validity of this, although female companion presents great resistance to sample takers. Suffice for the moment that not only has the cheddite projector been aligned to project the *Pleasantville Eagle,* within which it is installed, to a precise and distant spot, but it can take with the *Eagle* at least one hundred other ships."

"Chuckee thirstee," the almost brainless hulk muttered and struggled against the strap that held it to the chair. Jerry gave it a couple of inches of straight rye in a glass which soothed it somewhat.

"So the massive attack is planned and ready," Slug-Togath continued, "but could not begin until the precise location of secret laboratory was known. Since the first attack must blast straight to the lab and stop any attempt to escape with the cheddite projector there, nothing could be done until that information was obtained. Which, if you will pardon my saying so, X-9, is the purpose of our pres-

123

ence here and if you have the coordinates for the secret laboratory they would be greatly appreciated."

"83556.98 by 23976.23," the master spy instantly replied.

Slug-Togath wasted no time. He flipped the switches that hurled power into the ultlra-radio with the secret wavelength and, with a certain smugness in his voice said, "Slug-Togath reporting from Hagg-Loos. The coordinates of the secret laboratory are 83556.98 by 2396.23. Do you read me?"

They read him all right, for the results of his message were dramatic to say the least. The instant he had stopped speaking the sky above became black with Hagg-Inder battle cruisers, one hundred of them, instantly transported there across the gulf of space by the power of the cheddite projector. As soon as they had appeared, they roared into action, each hurtling toward an assigned target so that a moment later great explosions rocked the ground as ravening death hurled down from the wide-open projectors and guns of the fleet. Crackling bolts of electrical destruction tore at the national armory, the spaceport, the liquid lead works, the factories, the sewage plant, everything—for they showed no mercy. The very air crackled with the discharge of the mighty energies, and the solid earth beneath their claws trembled at its magnitude. Cautiously they lifted the manhole cover and peered out at the rain of destruction. But as they did so, some *force* grabbed onto X-9 and the robot Hagg-Loos and plucked them up into the air. Jerry and Slug-Togath both rushed to the weapons, but even as they touched the triggers, they saw the source of this strange force and relinquished their grips on the weapons. For they were being pulled straight up to the *Pleasantville Eagle,* which circled and swooped above. At the last moment, before they were crushed against the dural, the force lessened and drew them on, softly as a falling rising feather, to rest against the underside of the wing. They could see John waving from the pilot's compartment as his voice crackled on the radio.

"Welcome back, gang. As you can see, we were ready to go as soon as we got your message. We jumped here, and an automatic tracer zeroed in on your radio broadcast, and the new magnet beams, developed in the laboratories of the Hagg-Inder under the tutelage of the eons-old wisdom of the Garnishee, whisked you up. Now, so you don't think I'm just flying in circles and beating my gums, you will notice that below, as we talked, the gunner on the cheddite projector has been peeling back layer after layer of that immense fortress, hurling the layers into the sun of course, to expose the laboratory. Ahh, I believe that is it."

"It is indeed!" X-9 agreed, hurling the thought at them, since he had been telepathically following the conversation.

"Sic 'em!" Jerry jubilated as the flying fortress of the 747 dived like a hawk into the ruins. A light touch on the wheel, aided by a quick projection from the cheddite projector landed them right in the middle of the lab among the fleeing Hagg-Loos, a good number of whom were squashed by the wheels as they dropped.

Even as the wheels hit the combat doors (newly installed) dropped open, and from the cargo compartments roared weapon-wielding Hagg-Inder warriors, while from the cabin, no less roaring or weapon-wielding, came the Garnishee fighting men. Carnage was instantly spread among the benches. The ravening Hagg-Loos asked no quarter, nor would they grant it, fighting back with anything that came to hand, benches, crystal retorts, bars of metal, urinalysis samples; they were utterly fearless. But fearless, they died under the assault of the allies, who swept all before them.

"Would you kindly get us unstuck from this wing?" Jerry said, not too graciously as they thrashed impotently under the attraction of the magnet ray.

"Sorry about that," John apologized, cutting the power.

They dropped to the floor, and as they fell, Jerry saw a sight that made his blood run cold.

"Over there!" he bellowed into the microphone hooked to the external speakers. "Two of the crustacean swine are escaping with the cheddite projector. Stop them at all costs!"

Even as he spoke, the robot machine was hurling its mass across the room, plowing through any Hagg-Loos foolish enough to offer resistance. There were two of the enemy scientists carrying the machine, and one fell instantly to a lightning bolt from the forward gun. But the other, protected by the bulk of his fallen companion, dived for a secret door, pushing through it and closing it behind him. Jerry, in close pursuit, could not stop in time, and the machine plowed into the door with a horrible metallic clanging, then short-circuited. Electricity arced through the metal shell, and the occupants screamed sharply and leaped up as this same electricity raced through their metal chairs making a fundamental difference. An instant later the fighting warriors were there, dragging the disabled machine aside, battering down the door and rushing through the opening, led by the bellowing Lord Prrsi, who was shouting mighty oaths and war cries.

"There the blighter goes—tally-ho!" and the hunt streamed on.

But the moment's respite at the door had been enough for the fleeing Hagg-Loos scientist. He hurled himself and his precious burden into a monorail car that vanished into a tunnel mouth followed closely by bullets and blasts of energy.

"In a car heading due north," Lord Prrsi reported. "Pursuit impossible since this is the only car."

"North," Jerry mused as he struggled out of the ruined machine, and with Chuck following on the end of a string, Slug-Togath behind, he bounded athletically and hurriedly across the ruined laboratory and into the cool embrace of the *Pleasantville Eagle*. "North, that sounds familiar. Do you have a tracer on the cheddite?" he asked, sweat bursting from every pore.

"What has happened to Chuck!" Sally screamed, wringing her hands before the empty-eyed husk that had once been the man who loved her with every fiber of his being.

"Got him," John said, fingers rushing over the cheddite tracer controls. "Heading north at a great rate."

"Into the air and follow! I have a funny feeling that I know what is going on."

"Chuckee *hungry*," the husk muttered, and, through bloodshot, gummy eyes, it made out the round female form hand wringing before him. All those bumps meant something, the elusive memory was there—yes, it had it! "Chuckee hungry!" the husk bellowed and leaped, tearing Sally's clothes from her until she stood before them, naked except for the black wisp of her Maidenform bra and even wispier black panties.

"Enough of that, Chuck-thing," Jerry sighed and karated it into unconsciousness once more, then hopped around the room on one leg, sucking at his swollen karate hand which he had forgotten about. Sally vanished, screaming weakly, and they turned back to the more important business at hand.

"Due north," John said grimly. "I have a sneaking suspicion."

"So do I," Jerry agreed. "And isn't that an extinct volcano just coming into view?"

"The old ploy with the volcano and the spaceship," John laughed coldly. "But we have them this time. The instant it rockets into the air you get it with the cheddite projector, and *zingo!* end of the fiendish race of Lortonoi."

"You're on—and here it comes!" Jerry jammed his face against the viewfinder as smoke billowed from the mountain and a great spaceship hurled itself into view. He focused with a quick turn on the controls and jammed down on the firing button.

The Lortonoi ship vanished.

"You did it!" John shouted, slapping his comrade on the back with delight. "One blast, and there he went. What a shot!"

Jerry smiled sheepishly and covered his face with one hand and peered out between his fingers.

"Well, thanks, but you see, it didn't happen *quite* that way. It seems that the spacer vanished a millisecond before I pressed the button. Meaning. . . ."

"Don't elaborate, I get the message."

"Meaning that they have mastered the use of the cheddite projector and have fled with it, to wreak even further havoc through the civilized galaxy. But they'll not get away with it," he swore. "I have a tracer on them, and they are hopping with ten light-year jumps out *that* way, toward that cluster of stars. We'll fuel up and take off after them; we have no choice."

"And I will help," swore Slug-Togath, who had entered, "and my Garnishee warriors will follow as well."

"Not to mention the fact, chums, that we are ever so grateful on Hagg-Inder," came the beamed thought of Lord Prrsi. "Least we can do is pitch in and lend a hand, only civilized thing to do, you know."

"That's it!" Jerry exulted, smashing his fist into his palm and wincing. "That's it! Don't you see what that means? For the very first time in the eons-old history of the universe the civilized, intelligent races are banding together against evil, to combat it wherever it is found. A band of brothers, fighting together, dedicated to the pursuit of liberty, equality, and fraternity."

"I wouldn't exactly phrase it that way," Lord Prrsi commented. "I would rather say we are fighting for the maintenance of the class system and the continuancy of special privileges for the few."

"Call it what you want," Jerry shouted, "it is still democracy. Our gallant little band will go forth, fighting against any odds, pushing out the frontiers of liberty. We chosen, noble few will stand forth alone, just as the Texas Ranger did on the frontier of our land many years ago."

"You've said it, man," John broke in. "That's the word. Rangers. Rangers of space, combating evil wherever we find it."

"The Galaxy Rangers," Slug-Togath said in a hushed voice. "Where does an alien go to enlist?"

15

THEY SPEAK OF KRAKAR

The great royal hall of the Hagg-Inder was gay with bunting, colorful with noble decorations, slippery underfoot with the perspiration of the humanoid races who found that, even with the air conditioning turned full on, what proved to be a cold chill for the Hagg-Inder was a scorching furnace for them. But no one cared! Today was an important day, so important that it would go down in galactic history forever. Today the Galaxy Rangers officially came into being. The future Rangers thronged the floor, looking up at the dais where the king himself would pin on the first star of the first Ranger, number one, the lucky creature who would be commandant of the most powerful force for democracy that the lenticular galaxy had ever seen.

There had been a small difference of opinion on who the commandant would be. Since the *Pleasantville Eagle* and the cheddite projector, the backbone of the force for the Rangers, belonged to the four Earthlings, it had been decided that one of them would fill the top post. Sally was a simple girl, and Chuck was out of the running as well, his brain still no more active than a squashed watermelon despite the efforts of the finest Hagg-Inder brain men, so the choice naturally fell upon the remaining two. Jerry felt that since he had invented the cheddite projector, he should be number one, but it was pointed out to him that the guy who invented the *Monitor* had not been admiral of the Union Navy, so he grumbled into silence. As far as the other races could tell, the Earthlings were identical in abilities, and either would suit. In the end, a deadlock set in, with equal feelings—or lack of feelings—for both Jerry and John. Since the king was throwing out the first ball, the decision was left to him, and he chose John without an instant's thought.

"Discrimination," Jerry muttered to Sally where they sat sweating in the audience. "Just because he's black and they're black, they pick him without an instant's thought."

"But, Jerry, darling," she reasoned, "isn't it always like that? After all, on our tree-shaded, Midwest, bible belt, WASP campus wasn't John the only black and he was the janitor?"

He darted a suspicious look sideways out of narrowed brooding eyes. "What are you, a Commie or something?"

"Shhh—the king is about to speak."

A rustle of eager interest ran through the great hall on silent cat's feet and was replaced by a hushed silence as the king clattered slowly forward.

"Hagg-Inder, Earthlings, Garnishee, strange-looking creatures of many races. My mate and I wish to announce, upon this auspicious occasion, the founding of the soon-to-be-historical, instantly galaxy famous organization by the name of. . . ." He blinked his faceted eyes at a metallic sheet on the stand before him. "An organization by the name of the Galaxy Rangers."

Instant pandemonium filled the great hall as cheer after cheer split the red-hot air. It took a long time for the enthusiasm to die down, and the king could only be heard after portions of the floor under the noisiest spectators had been electrified.

"With this bold band of brothers formed, the next need is for a gallant leader to lead these gallant warriors and, after careful democratic selection"—a single angry snort was ignored—"the Earthling John was nominated unanimously for this signal honor, and it is my privilege to present him with badge number one of the Galaxy Rangers."

There were more cheers as John stepped forward and the king pinned the golden star upon his chest. John screamed hoarsely as the king ran three inches of pointed steel wire in John's pectoral muscle since, in the heat of the moment, he had forgotten that aliens *pinned* the pin to their clothing instead of drilling a hole in the chitin for attaching these kind of things. With shaking fingers John

130

finished pinning on the golden star with the large number 1 upon it, the words "Galaxy Rangers" picked out neatly in diamonds, and turned to the microphone, blood seeping a ruddy patch into his clean white shirt.

"Fellow Rangers, I greet you. I am going personally to pin Ranger star number two upon my old friend, Jerry Courteney, and after that it is *your* turn. Don't fight as you rush forward; there are stars enough for all. What an opportunity this is! Travel, education, career, the job of your choice, free medical and dental attention, and that can mean a lot—like, for instance, that alien there with more teeth than a piano keyboard, he'll really make out. This is the opportunity of a lifetime. We are here creatures of many different races; I count among the escaped prisoners from the DnDrf mines at least forty different species and who knows how many offspring from mixed marriages, all eager to join up. As further inducement to enlist, I mention the fact that we have no transport to take you back to your home worlds, and as soon as we Galaxy Rangers take off, the Hagg-Inder turn off the air conditioning and, zowie, it's two hundred and fifty degrees again. But don't let me attempt to pressure you in my enthusiasm. Let your conscience be your guide. And form a single line to the right, and anyone who doesn't want to come can just stay here and sweat it out. For, ha-ha, a long time."

To a man, or really to an alien, they volunteered, and the Galaxy Rangers were already making a mark in history. But all was not happiness. Later, after the exhausting ceremonies, the Earthlings were sitting in the first-class lounge of the *Pleasantville Eagle*, having cocktails and chopped Ormoloo liver and facing one inescapable fact.

"He's got about as much intelligence as a damp kitchen mop," Jerry said, nodding to his old buddy Chuck, who sat on the floor chewing happily on a shoelace and mumbling to himself.

"Could the Hagg-Inder physicians do nothing?" Sally implored.

John shook his head in an unhappy no. "They did their best, their top people, super mind readers and all that. Too far gone, they say, for their meager talents."

"And their meager talents are the best in the galaxy," Jerry brooded. "So I guess we ought to start thinking about euthanasia next, as soon as we are sure about his will."

"You cannot!" gasped Sally.

"Why not! If he's going to sit around and drool like that for maybe fifty years more, he is not much good to anyone, including himself."

"You are so cruel!"

"I am not. I'll bet you that Chuck would want it that way. I certainly would if it came to the choice."

"I say, not interrupting anything am I?" Lord Prrsi asked, poking one great faceted eye into the room.

"Nothing important," Sally snapped. "Just murder and such."

"Well, yes, indeed. Then I'll just slip in and curl in the corner and turn my heater on high. Yes, thank you, I would appreciate one, very tasty." He smacked loudly as he drained a gallon of dry martini at a gulp. "I've come here rather unofficially, so to speak, and would appreciate it if what I tell you stayed inside these four walls. Or would it be six if you counted ceiling and floor?"

"Prrsi, old sting-tail," Jerry said, "we are not in the mood to discuss state secrets at the present time, I hope you'll understand. We are discussing the fate of our incapacitated comrade Chuck."

"Well, so am I, old fruit. But what I propose is highly illegal and dangerous."

"What is it?" the three friends asked, leaning forward as one.

"Well now. Hear me out, I beg, before interrupting. The tale I have to tell may sound strange, but I heartily assure you, it is true, though a well-kept secret. Far to the south of here just beyond Averno Desert are a range of sharp hills that the local peasants call the Mountains of Madness. Many people who venture into them are never heard of again. Many years ago the then king sent an expedition into the hills, armed, tough-minded Hagg-Inder, utterly fearless, sneering at alien or beast. They were gone for months, all track lost. Finally, a single survivor, chitin

132

scratched and filthy, crawled into a village just beyond the mountains. He would not speak of what had occurred, and the peasants were not that interested in hearing the details in any case. But he was brought here and spoke with the king and the nobles, and since that time we in the royal house know about it but don't say a word."

"About what?" Jerry asked, completely confused.

"Didn't I ask you not to interrupt?" Lord Prrsi said peevishly, lashing his poison barb back and forth and rattling his claws on the walls. They were silent. "Well, to go on, if you *don't* mind. The secret has been kept ever since. In those mountains, in a certain valley, lives one of our race, an ancient of uncountable years. He lives in a cave by himself, a hermit mystic who does not wish to be disturbed as he thinks his centuries-old thoughts. If anyone comes close, he blasts their mind with a mind blast of such intensity that it cannot be averted. Now, as you know, our race has great mental powers, second only to the foul Lortonoi, and even against them we can hold our own. This will give you some idea of the mental strength of the hermit. Word of the mind blasting is common in the area, so of course, few venture that way. But before he died, the sole survivor told us that the hermit does not blast minds just like that. He asks the potential mind blastee three questions or riddles, and if they are answered, why, then the prisoner goes free."

"What has that got to do with us?" asked Sally. "I don't want my mind blasted."

"Goodness, no one would want to blast your sweet little mind, Earthling female. If I might continue. Now it seems that one of the party had been struck on the head by a fallen boulder and his chitin crushed in and his brains pretty well mashed to boot. He was being taken back for medical treatment, although all there agreed that his case was hopeless. But it wasn't! The hermit, with the incredible strength of his thoughts, restored the hapless victim to normality before asking the questions. His brain was so good he even got two of them right, though he muffed the third and had his restored brain instantly blasted."

"I see," Jerry mused. "But it's a long chance."

"It's the only chance," John said.

The silence stretched as the two men looked each other in the eye; then it stretched some more.

"Well, I'll go if you won't," Sally said, springing to her feet. "Can you get me a map, Prrsi?"

"Ahh, you are indeed a stout brick, little Earthling chum. But, hope you won't mind my saying it, it will take a far sturdier mind than yours to stand up to that of the hermit. It will need a mind of at least seven hundred and forty-three IQ, a genius, a person of great moral fiber and strength, a natural-born leader, one healthily oversexed."

"That's me," John and Jerry said, with one voice, standing at attention, volunteering, not realizing how well they had been conned by the cool brain of the red-hot alien.

Before they really realized what they had become involved in, they were in heatproof suits, stuffing the protesting Chuck into one as well, waving good-bye to Sally and rushing out of the city in a great tractor-treaded vehicle with Lord Prrsi at the wheel.

"We didn't bring much in the way of supplies," Jerry grumbled.

"Either way, this trip won't take long," Lord Prrsi said breezily.

"Gee, thanks," John muttered, and they settled down to a day and a night of uncomfortable boredom. The powerful machine tore across the desert, the untiring Prrsi at the controls, sending up an immense cloud of dust from its treads. When night fell, glaring headlights of piercing actinic light speared through the darkness and their pace never slowed. At noon, on the second day, they raced toward a range of mountains that had been growing steadily before them, and Lord Prrsi braked to a squealing stop at the mouth of a narrow canyon.

"I don't imagine you chaps can feel them, with your rudimentary powers, but I have been fighting mental waves of great intensity for the last couple of hours, attempting to turn me away. Instead, I have followed them to their source, this canyon. I am afraid I must let you out here, for I dare not go on. Take your hopelessly incapacitated friend and proceed. I wish you the best of luck."

"An atomic pistol would be a lot more help," Jerry said ingratiatingly.

"Weapons are forbidden in the valley. To possess them means instant death. I will wait for you here. Farewell."

Step by hesitant step, the brave Earthmen climbed up through the crumbling scree, leading the Chuck-thing at the end of a leash. It was hard going, and they had to stop to rest many times and suck at the nipples of the water tanks inside their helmets. They neither saw nor heard anything out of the ordinary, though both were possessed by a feeling of immense dread. A wave of depression against which they had to push physically. But they *pushed* because they were that kind of men, now having to carry the screeching, brainless Chuck forcefully. Finally, before a sharp turn in the narrow valley, there came a mental blast that almost seared out their synapses, a mental command that said but one thing.

"STOP!"

They stopped, frozen, unable to move, even Chuck paralyzed by the intensity of the command. Then a voice spoke to them, or rather a mental voice spoke within their own minds, and they heard it louder than they had ever heard any sound with their ears.

"LEAVE HERE WHILE YOU ARE STILL ALIVE!"

"We have come this far, we will not turn back," Jerry said staunchly. "And would you mind turning the volume down?" When the voice spoke to them again, it was still loud, but bearable.

"You know that there is no return from this valley of death unless the Test is passed? And few pass it."

"We know that, but we have come for our friend's sake. If we pass the test, we sort of hoped—"

"No bargains! I will decide what is to be done. Come forward."

Their feet almost did not obey them as they shuffled forward against the mounting wave of mental dread that filled the valley. Around the turn they staggered and stopped, without willing it, below a shelf that lay just in front of the black opening of a cave. They *knew* it was in

135

that cave, even if the skulls and skeletons scattered on the ground before it were not a dead giveaway.

"I am called Baksheesh, and all who have come here have feared me!"

"Well, here are three more, Mr. Baksheesh," Jerry gasped, knees trembling despite everything he did, chilled and shivering despite the 240-degree temperature outside their suits.

"Are you prepared for the question?"

"We are." John shivered in response.

"Then you are first. You have ten seconds to answer the following. . . ."

"Hey, you didn't mention any time limit before this."

A cold chuckle was his only answer. *"Prepare now. We play this game by my rules since it is my game. Ready. What is black and deadly and sits in a tree?"*

John tightened his forehead in concentration as the seconds ticked away, gleefully counted off by the murderous Baksheesh. Jerry leaned over and tried to whisper, but a blast of mental energy blew up a boulder next to him.

"None of that or the mind blast blasts right now."

"Sorry, I didn't know coaching was against the rules."

"It is now. Seven . . . eight . . . nine. . . ."

"I have it! A crow with a machine gun."

A wave of miffed mental radiation swept over them and was instantly gone. *"Think you're so smart!"* the mental voice muttered. *"So let's see how well your buddy does on the next one. Five seconds on this one. And miss one question and you all die."*

Jerry steeled himself, tightening his muscles and thinking healthy thoughts to clean his brain. "Ready when you are, Baksheesh," he said. And back came the mental blast with the question.

"What looks like a box, smells like a lox—and flies? Five . . . four. . . ." It was counting faster now. *"Three . . . two. . . ."*

"A flying lox box!" Jerry shouted defiantly, and the muttering wave of mental anger in reply told him that he was right.

"That's two out of three, but it's anyone's ball game yet.

I'm going to ask your drooling friend there the next question. . . ."

"But you can't! He's not human. His mind has been chopped up by the vile Lortonoi."

"Hmmm, yes, so it has. And a sloppy job too, just like them. Here, I'll lift this mental block, erase that pattern, pour another in here, tap this subconscious memory and drain it into the right lobe. There, he's as good as new, maybe better. Now my question. . . ."

"Hold on," John called out. "We don't know if you have really fixed his brain; you may just be saying that. We'll have to talk to him first."

His words were cut off by a bone-chilling cackle of shrill laughter.

"My rules, remember? Now, Chuck-thing, you have one second to answer the following question. Ready now, think. What is the square of the product of 456.78 times 923.45 divided by 65.23 plus 92565.286? The answer?"

"99031.75 is the product to two decimal places, and the square of that number is, dropping the decimal places for the moment, 980713896. Do you want it with the decimal places too?"

A mentally muttered morbid curse was his only answer, and Chuck smiled warmly as his two friends came forward to beat him on the back and welcome him back to sanity.

"I was going to ask you what we were doing here. The last I remember is some torture or other and things getting dim; then, bango, I'm in this valley and somebody asked me that question, and by reflex of course, I put the old brain box to work and dug up the answer. I was startled so it was a good thing it was a simple question."

"That's about enough of the old self-laudatory praise," the voice spoke coldly in their minds. Not only in their minds, but they realized suddenly that they were hearing it with their ears. They looked up at the ledge whence the voice had spoken and recoiled together. For there was Baksheesh.

He was an ancient, gnarled, scratched and generally beat-up native of the planet Haggis, that was obvious. But he was *old*. Generations of spiders had built webs between

137

his claws until he was almost wrapped in a cocoon. Yet for all his age, the light of a great intelligence burned in his crystalline eyes. Nor was that all. His color. . . .

"White. I know what you are thinking," the thought crackled down at them. *"Hideous white like the vile Hagg-Loos, not beautiful and black like the Hagg-Inder. Well, I have news for you. I AM a Hagg-Loos. Ha! You might very well cringe back at that news. But I am above petty politics now. Once I was as human as any other, and as mad as any, but the fortunes of war brought me here, and I crawled into that cave and came to rest over a powerful radioactive source. My madness was cured, and my intelligence soared as I was made immortal by most standards. Including my own, I must add. But to remain immortal I must toast over the radioactives. If I leave the cave, I die, so now I must return. You know my secret, but you will not betray me, for my wisdom is of the ages. I have come before you to tell you one thing that you must never forget."* It rattled its antenna wildly, and the last thought blasted like a hurricane through their minds.

"BEWARE THE KRAKAR!"

They staggered under the mental blast, and when they looked up, the pallid creature had gone, and they were alone among the bones and chitin of the dead.

16

ENIGMA IN SPACE

"Krakar . . . Krakar . . . now where did I hear that before?"

Lord Prrsi muttered to himself, trying to place the transient memory that rattled around inside the chitin of his head. This was at the meeting of the top executives of the Galaxy Rangers, and they were having this first historical meeting in the first-class lounge of the *Pleasantville Eagle*. Sally, who had been made president of the Ladies' Auxiliary and given a gold brooch with a miniature star on it, was serving drinks while the Rangers discussed the fateful final words spoken by Baksheesh. Sally passed around cigars, and most of the Earthmen lit up, though Jerry was enjoying a joint, and the aliens present either ate theirs or threw them under the chairs when no one was looking.

"I have it!" Lord Prrsi shouted and snapped his claws in excitement, cutting a solid steel lounge chair in half without noticing it. "Somewhere in the transcript from one of the Hagg-Loos prisoners we took when we raided their secret laboratory. Just hold on, chaps, I'll send a mental command to the computer to dig it out and beam it back to me. Won't take long."

John rapped for attention with his whiskey glass, then held it up to Sally for a refill.

"While we're waiting for that thought to come through, let's hear that security report that old squid-head Slug-Togath put together on the Lortonoi. You have the floor, Sluggy."

The Garnishee prime minister rose and coughed with two or three of his mouths, then picked up the report with the tentacles on his head and held it before a couple of his close-reading eyes. He coughed again and began.

"This is an amalgamation of all information that could

be obtained about our traditional and mentally repulsive enemy, the brain-sucking Lortonoi. Evidence was taken from every race that has fought the Lortonoi, and more evidence tortured out of those who have fought cheek by jowl with these disgusting creatures. The first fact we have uncovered is that no one, not even their allies, has ever seen a Lortonoi. They arrive in their own spaceship and hardly ever leave it, since all instructions and commands are given by mental telepathy. On certain occasions, as in the secret laboratory of the Hagg-Loos, they have made an appearance, but since they arrived in a great armored tank and never left it, this isn't much help either."

"So you've told us what we don't know," John said. "What *do* we know?"

"I'm just getting to that part. We know that they have fantastic mental powers which they use only for evil. They appear at many places through the galaxy and aid any race they can either mentally control or which is nasty enough to go along with them. In their travels they seem to have picked up a knowledge of all the weapons and science that are around, so that any race they aid immediately goes to war with any other race nearby. Very nasty. Their goal seems to be complete control of the galaxy for their own evil ends."

"And ours is to crush them for free enterprise, a rigid class system and all the other forms of democracy we love," John shouted, and all present cheered. "Now what about it, Lord Prrsi, you old red-hot scorpion, any word yet from your molasses-clogged computer? Seems pretty slow."

"Really quite fast, Number One. The answer came back within three nanoseconds, but I didn't want to interrupt the pep talk. It seems that while we were questioning one of the technicians, he shouted something like 'The Krakar will get you, ha-ha' before he lapsed into a coma."

"Coma?"

"Understandable. Our questioning can be rather severe at times, but after all, they are only Hagg-Loos, and working class at that."

"Can you get any more out of him?" Jerry asked. "Maybe even a spot of torture if you have to."

"My dear boy! What on Haggis do you think our normal questioning is? Short of stripping off his chitin and boiling him like a lobster, there is little else we can do. He is still recovering from the last round of questioning, and I sincerely doubt that more of the same will reveal any more than this. Very strong-willed, these blighters, and insane to boot."

"Why don't you try curing his madness?" Sally asked, refilling the glasses, but they went on talking, ignoring her completely. Jerry was holding forth in great detail on Earthly torture methods to see if the Hagg-Inder had missed any when she raised the glass martini jug and dropped it onto his head. Well, this caught their attention a bit, and while she had it, she repeated her question. "Why don't you try curing the prisoner's insanity and perhaps he will cooperate voluntarily?"

"Bourgeois sentimentality!" Lord Prrsi snorted.

"Did you have to do that?" Jerry said aggrievedly, picking a pickled onion out of his ear.

"I think you might have an idea there, Sally." John rapped again for order. "What about it, Prrsi you old sting-tail monster? Why don't you have your shrinks try to cure this guy, put a metal box around his brain so he doesn't have a relapse, read to him from the Bible, the Magna Carta and the Declaration of Independence. . . ."

"Fill his head with that subversive rot!"

"Sure, you can always kill him afterward so the word doesn't spread, but it might work."

"I say, it might indeed. I'll issue an order by thought mail . . . there, it's gone. Work will begin at once."

"All right, then to new business," John said. "Work on our secret Ranger base on Planet X, tenth planet of this sun Sirius, has been completed and we can move our volunteers there so the Hagg-Inder can turn off their air conditioning."

"Well, thank Great Cacodyl!" Lord Prrsi breathed. "I swear I am turning blue-black from the cold and feel gal-

141

loping pneumonia coming on. Anything below the boiling point of water gives me a positive chill on my liver."

"Save the medical chitchat for later," John said. "Let's get on with this so we can get down to some heavy drinking, and listen, Jerry, that is the third joint in a quarter hour, and your eyes are getting glassy. Can you kindly hold off a bit, huh? So, more business. We sent a spy team in a fast battle cruiser to scout out the star cluster where the Lortonoi headed when they escaped last time. Just for a change we shouldn't go off half-cocked racing around the stars without a bit of look-see first. While we are waiting for their report, we are consolidating our position, building our base, getting more volunteers by capturing slave ships and that kind of thing. It also gives us some time to look into this Krakar thing, which has a very nasty sound to it, before we get involved in more fighting, that is, and it turns out that the Lortonoi are going to give *us* the Krakar, right in the old you-know-where."

"I'll second that motion," Chuck said. "Krakar must be solved."

The medical teams went to work. Utilizing their great mental skills, as well as some Earthling techniques like aversion therapy, prefrontal lobotomy, shock treatment, dianetic auditing, and the psychoanalytic couch, they did a quick cure on the laboratory technician. As soon as he was sane, he saw the error of his ways and voluntarily told everything he knew. Everything turned out to be something, but not very much: the spatial coordinates of the place where Krakar was supposed to be and the interesting information that whoever controlled Krakar controlled the galaxy.

"Let's go," Jerry shouted, rubbing his hands together. "Blast in, full force, take 'em by surprise, atomize the enemy, grab Krakar, and the galaxy is ours!"

"Best not to go off half-cocked," Chuck mused. "Whatever that means."

"I know," Sally said. "A historical expression relating to the early weapons that had a flint and steel and were cocked—"

142

"Shut up," Jerry hinted. "If you have a better idea, Chuck old man—why, let us hear it."

"I think we ought to have a quick scout first to see what we are getting into and to find out maybe what Krakar is. If it could be grabbed by force that easily, you can bet the Lortonoi would have done it long before this. Just us Earthmen, and Sally along for cooking, and we shouldn't be away more than a day or two."

"Great, Chuck," John agreed. "Sort of a holiday, and we deserve it."

"And I deserve permanent KP?" Sally asked, but no one was listening.

Soon the faithful *Pleasantville Eagle* was ready and rarin' to go. Fuel tanks filled, oxygen brimming over, guns loaded, bar restocked. With Jerry at the controls they made great ten-light-year leaps toward their destination. There was a newly mounted electronic superscope in the ship's nose that threw a highly magnified picture onto a screen, and Chuck was at the controls.

"Nothing," he mused. "Yet we are almost to the center of the star cluster where Krakar is supposed to be. Are you sure we haven't got the wrong figures or something?"

"Negative," John said, going through the tech reports. "We have carefully plotted the spatial directions eight ways from Sunday and to one hundred and thirteen decimal places. Krakar *has* to be near here somewheres. I tell you what, make another jump, a teensy jump, maybe just a couple of light-years this time, no more than 1,671,321,600,000 nautical miles, which is two light-years."

"Here we go."

They jumped—and instantly every alarm in the ship blasted an earsplitting cacophony as they appeared almost in the shadow of a fantastically huge space battleship that was at least a mile long. Widemouthed gunports were ranged the length of its deadly gray metal hide, and it reeked of an overpowering air of efficient destruction. Jerry jabbed at the button that would jump them out of there, but before his thumb could touch it, mighty magnet

143

beams locked onto the great form of the 747, a mosquito compared to an eagle now, and instantly whisked it up against the pocked metal skin of the ship. Paralyzer rays flooded the ship, and they could not move. At the same moment a jointed metal tube shot out from the battleship, and a device on the end, very much resembling an electric can opener, buzzed noisily in a circle, and a section of hull fell clanging inside the plane. Zombie rays must have been operating as well because they all stood, despite their every effort to resist, and they marched slowly into the cabin to stand ranked before the ragged opening. Heavy footsteps clumped down the tube toward them, and their hands all flashed up to their temples in a snappy salute.

"At ease," said the creature who entered, and their arms dropped. "Name of ship, planet of origin, defensive armament, passports of crew, VD rate. Report."

They could only gape. The alien was tremendous, standing over eight feet tall and glowering down at them. It had short, solid legs and a long, thick body, which it needed since it had four arms on each side, or eight in all. It wore a neatly cut uniform of dark black—what a tailor he must have had!—and a black helmet on its head. The head! Eight red eyes gleamed in a row below the helmet's lip, while below them was a nose shaped like a vacuum cleaner hose. To complete this singularly repulsive picture, his wide mouth was filled to overflowing with black teeth, most of which protruded like tusks at interesting angles.

"Report!" it shouted, waving a clipboard it carried in one hand, a short sword, a pistol, a club, and lots of other things in its other hands, and it still had a couple of hands free to shake fists at them.

Jerry reported. Listing everything they had, though he did manage to forget the cheddite projector, their only big secret.

"Haven't you forgot something?" Sally said brightly, "The ched—"

She wasn't sure who had given her the knee from behind so efficiently, but it stopped her. The ugly alien turned a couple of eyes her way.

"She means the cheddar cheese in the galley, the bagels,

144

the baked beans and other food supplies, but you don't want to hear about that, no!" John said brightly.

For an instant of time that seemed to stretch to eternity the alien glared down at them, his eyes seeming to probe their innermost thoughts. Finally, it spoke, in a deep nasty rumble.

"Split. If you aren't moving out of here at top speed within two seconds after we release the magnetic rays, you will be blasted into infinitesimal fragments."

"Wait a minute!" Jerry shouted angrily. "You can't talk to us like that. . . ."

"Oh, *yes*, I can."

"Well, you can talk to us like that if you want to. But can't you at least explain what is happening?"

"What is happening, as if you didn't know, ugly too-few-eyes, too-few-arms alien, is that you are in the outer shell of the attacking forces that have been attacking the Chachkas for the past two hundred and eighty-five years. We always welcome recruits to the fighting forces since a certain amount of fighting equipment is used up, and volunteers are accepted, and in proportion to their contribution of arms a similar percentage will be given in the occupied galaxy, which we will control as soon as we have Krakar—"

"What *is* Krakar?"

"Who knows? Except we know that it is written that he who controls it controls the galaxy, and that is what we aim to do. Your aim too, but you missed. Your strength is too slight to get even an infinitesimal cut of the galaxy, so now beat it. Your time has run out."

The alien spun about on one thick heel and started for the exit.

"Do you take bribes?" Chuck called after it.

It spun about, weapons raised, and Sally fainted. For one eternal moment it stood there rattling its prominent teeth and death hovered low in the air.

"Of course I take bribes," it gnashed. "Doesn't everybody? Make me an offer."

"What do you want? Diamonds, gold, greenbacks,

vodka, dirty books, jet fuel, oxygen, Hershey bars? You name it, we got it."

"I spit on your dirty books, not enough arms for fun, but a cupful of diamonds will see me through until payday. What do you want in exchange?"

"Just a chance to get into the fighting zone and let fly with all our weapons at the enemy; then we will head for home."

"Won't do any harm—and I can use the loot. Pour them into this pocket," he said to Chuck who had gone to the safe and returned with a measuring cup full of blue-whites. The alien scratched quickly on the clipboard and tore off a chit and handed it to them. "Here's your clearance and coordinates. Get in there, fire your load, and be out within ten minutes or you have had it, buddy. That's as far as this tiny bribe goes."

"Eternally at your service, sir," Jerry called after the retreating back as they lifted the ragged disk of metal into position and welded it back into place before they lost all of their atmosphere. The tube was sucked back into the battleship and they floated free.

"I'm using the space warper drive to get us into position," Chuck said, spinning the controls. "We'll save the cheddite projector for an emergency, for if they have any clue to its existence, they will tear the ship apart upon the instant. Hold tight, folks, here we go."

Space warped and was penetrated, and they appeared suddenly notched into position in a great globe of ships in space. As far as they could see in every direction, spaceships of every size and shape floated in this hollow globe formation and released a storm of weaponry at the object floating at the mathematical center of this sphere in space. It was hard to see just what was down there because of the fury of attack, the scintillating rays, the destructive vibrating beams, the explosive filled torpedoes and high-powered shells that were continuously rained down upon the target. They put on dark glasses and finally made out a golden sphere at the heart of all the activity. It could not have been more than a mile in diameter, yet it withstood the ravening might of the greatest engines of destruction

146

ever assembled in the lenticular galaxy. And it fought back. Occasionally a thin red beam of light would lash up from the golden surface, and anything it touched instantly exploded with terrible effect. Entire ships went up this way, and one five-mile-long battleship bought it while they watched, blowing up so efficiently that it took four other ships with it in the explosion. Yet instantly, ships waiting in the second sphere filled the gaps, and the battle went on.

"Whoever is down there sure has plenty on the ball," John breathed, speaking for them all.

"Just two minutes left," Jerry said, eying the chronometer.

"I'll bet you have the same idea I have." Chuck laughed.

"And me too," agreed John.

"Right on! We set our coordinates exactly and appear inside that sphere with our trusty old bird here. All their weapons are pointed *away* from the golden sphere. If we get inside, the place will be ours, and *we'll* have Krakar!"

"No!" Sally begged. "It is sure suicide. How can we weak Earthlings accomplish what the combined might of this alien space armada cannot?"

"That's just the point," Jerry answered, and the others nodded agreement. "It just goes to show you that we are a lot better than them with their big battleships and extra arms and teeth and things. Give me a good old Earthman any day! Right, gang?"

Sally was brushed aside, and to enthusiastic cheers, the suicidally inclined men set the cheddite projector, calibrating it exactly at the center of the sphere, then pressed the actuating button just as their time was up.

17

LO! SUCH WONDERS
STAND REVEALED

There was a quick flick, and the scene changed—but
really changed. An unmeasurable instant before they had
been in interstellar space, part of the immense fleet that
was attacking the golden globe. Now they were inside the
globe, they had to be. So the plan had worked!

The *Pleasantville Eagle* had appeared inside the space
construction maybe a couple of feet above the floor. Now
it fell and bounced in its undercarriage and its passengers
bounced off each other, the lucky ones bouncing off Sally,
who was by far the most pneumatic. There was a crash of
broken glass from the galley; then everything was still.

"Just look out there, will you!" Chuck enthused,
pointing. "I have a feeling that we were not expected."

It appeared that they were not. They were in the middle
of an immense chamber whose curved walls were covered
with hulking machines of incomprehensible design, all
made of gold. There were many viewscreens and controls
among the machinery, and small creatures were at these
controls; they were too far away to make out details, but
they certainly had a nasty look. While they were taking in
the details and strapping on loaded guns, Sally began to
tremble and moan and salivate a bit. Chuck looked at her,
then slapped his forehead with the heel of his hand.

"Too late," he said. "Remember, guys, how we all put
on mind shields before we came here so our minds would
be shielded. Well, you remember Sally had to comb her
hair. . . . Yeah, I guess her mind shield is still in her
purse."

Instantly all the guns pointed at her as she shivered,
then began to speak in a deep and resonant voice.

"You aliens may leave, and we will not harm you, for you are trespassing on our domain."

"Try again," Jerry sneered for all of them.

"This is simple research satellite, nothing more."

"You're lying, aren't you?" John said.

"Yes, I am lying," Sally said hoarsely, and her shoulders slumped. "We Chachkas can tell only the truth, and I will never live down the shame of telling that lie. In fact . . . it is too much . . . I cannot bear it, living with the shame. Good-bye, fellow Chachkas, good-bye, ugly soft aliens. It is a far, far better thing I do than I have ever done . . . *arrrgh!*"

Sally swayed and almost fell, but before they could reach her, she pulled herself erect again and spoke in an even deeper voice.

"Chachka Two has committed suicide, so I, Chachka Three take command. You must leave—"

"Listen," Chuck broke in. "We don't like to deal with the hired help. Put Chachka One on the line."

"Would that I could, he was a friend to us all. But he was crossing the floor when your monster machine appeared and dropped on him. One leg can be seen projecting from under your right front wheel."

"Accidents happen," John consoled him. "In any case we are here, and this is the moment of truth. So speak. You are the guardians of Krakar, aren't you?"

"We are," Sally intoned. "Carrying on our eons-old destiny. You see before you the last descendants of the Chachka, the oldest race in the lenticular galaxy. We were old when your planet was young. While the great saurians wallowed in the swamps of Earth, our empire was at its zenith, stretching from star to star, spanning the universe. We were mighty, and yet we fell, for the lesser races were jealous of our power and warred against us, and the wars grew more and more ferocious. But with age comes wisdom, and when, almost at the end, the ultimate weapon was invented, reason prevailed and it was never used. We retreated instead, from planet to planet, signing humbling peace agreements, until we had retreated to the solar system whence we had sprung. Then a racial rot set in, for we who had been so strong were now so humble, and youngsters were not born and the fields fell into disuse and we were doomed. Our race, you might say, died of a broken heart."

"Then what are you doing here now?" Jerry asked.

"If you'll shut up, I'll tell you. I was just getting to the best part. You see, having discovered the ultimate weapon and then not using it gave the best minds in our race a real mental lift. Most races think they are better than all the others; it just so happened that we knew it. So this golden sphere was constructed, holding within it the best of all the science we had ever known. Into it also went the best minds of the race to carry on the great work we had begun. It was agreed that just because we had no real need to use the ultimate weapon did not mean that at some future date there might not arise a situation where it might have to be used. Therefore, we watch and wait, but to date we have seen no occasion to even consider cracking it out of cold storage."

"And the name of the ultimate weapon is Krakar?" John asked.

"It is. Very bright of you. All the races that have heard of it have come here with lust and murder burning within them and have attempted to take it by force."

"Not us," John said, letting his gunbelt drop to the floor so he could kick it under a chair. "We have nothing but peace within our hearts, we Galaxy Rangers, and have devoted our all to the destruction of the Lortonoi, who are dedicated to taking over the galaxy for their own slimy ends. We can sure use your old Krakar, so why not hand it over?"

"Never!" Sally swayed. "We see the guns and cannons and the rest of the crap sticking out of your winged machine, not so peaceful that. No, we have to be convinced before we turn Krakar over to anyone. And we are geared to defend ourselves. You see how little effect those ships out there have upon our indestructible sphere. We are surrounded by a wall of energy that cannot be penetrated."

"Well, *we* got in," Chuck said, proudly. "So your defenses aren't all that darned good."

"We are aware of that. Your cheddite projector is a simple variation of our R-Shi, ray, which we discarded eons ago as a childish toy, then forgot about it."

"Too bad," Jerry said, looking at his fingernails, then polishing them on his sleeve. "You should have kept it around, and then we wouldn't be inside here now and sort of insisting that you turn over Krakar to us."

"Even that contingency has been considered. If any attempt is made to take Krakar in this fashion, any one of our race can press an instant destruct button that blows everything up. Krakar and the works will be gone forever. We would rather do that than have it fall into the wrong hands."

"Sort of stalemate," John mused. "Look, why don't we sit down around a conference table like intelligent life forms and see what we can work out? And besides, Sally is going to have a sore throat after all this."

"We are amenable," Three said after a moment's thought. "Would you be kind enough to leave your weapons behind when you emerge? You will find that our atmosphere is breathable by primitive creatures like yourselves. Over and out." Sally staggered and clutched at her neck. "Christ, my throat hurts!" she grated.

While Sally gargled with salt water, the rest of the Earthlings dumped their weapons and exited. Three was waiting at the foot of the gangway to greet them. "Welcome," he said in the familiar deep voice.

"Well I'll be hornswoggled." Chuck gaped for all of them. "These Chachkas look just like foot-long, black cockroaches with little pink hands on their front feet!"

"Yes, and you humans look like great, soft gop-worms that used to live in our swamps and ate by standing on their heads and sucking in mud. Now if we can drop the racial slander, we can get on with the business at hand. While you were making your clumsy way out of your archaic vehicle, I had a conference with the other leaders. Since we can think about a hundred times faster than you primitive forms, you might say we had a day-long rap session and we have reached a conclusion. We have nothing against you, other than you look like gop-worms, that is, but we only hand over Krakar for like a real galaxy-wide emergency. So far you haven't convinced us. What *might* convince us is a complete knowledge of your antecedents, history, moral turpitude, intelligence, sexual deviations, culture, etc. If we had this we could decide if the present emergency justifies the use of Krakar."

"You're not asking very much," John told him. "We could be here ten years and not supply all the info you need."

"That is where you are wrong, primitive softling. If you permit us, we can make an instant print of *all* your memories, including your racial memories, and with that we can make a true evaluation in a couple of minutes more. Do you agree?"

"What do we have to do?" Chuck asked suspiciously for all of them.

"Just agree, that's all, since we Chachkas are not only incredibly honest but cannot take anything by force, including a memory. If you agree, why then brain-copying rays will instantly lash down, penetrating easily those primitive mind shields, and make a copy of everything you have lurking in the old gray matter. You will feel nothing."

"Well, what do you say, guys?" Jerry asked. The others thought for a moment, then nodded agreement. "Okay, you can do it, Three."

"It's already done. I told you it wouldn't hurt. Now, while the memories are being processed, may I offer you a little refreshment? We have a fine hundred-year-old Napoleon brandy, manufactured instantly from your memories by our reconstitutor machines and indistinguishable from the original. Try it."

They managed to work the ancient cork out and poured a golden measure into each snifter, then smacked and gasped and moaned with delight.

"Keep the bottle, I don't drink," Three said with an

offhand wave of its tentacle. "Ahh, the results are coming through. My, oh, my, you do have some loathsome material well sublimated in your subconscious minds, but that is neither here nor there. What is interesting is that the Lortonoi might very well be the galaxy-wide menace that Krakar will be needed to destroy, so you boys are in luck."

"Then we get the weapon?" John asked, leaning forward expectantly.

"You do not. Didn't you hear the operative *might* in that sentence? What we will do is give you an instant communicator that will enable you to contact us instantly from any part of the galaxy. If the situation is so desperate that it looks as if the Lortonoi are going to take over, you have simply to drop us the word, then press your head against the device. We'll make a memory copy to get up to date and decide then."

"Is that your best offer?" Jerry asked.

"Best offer we have made in a little over eight billion years, so consider yourself lucky. The communicator is now resting within your machine. So take it and leave and good riddance. Oh, yes, one thing before you go. Our incredible machinery is powered by a matter destruction generator that generates energy by the total destruction of matter. We will be running out of mass to burn in it in about a couple of hundred years. Just to be sure, we would like to have some extra on hand. If you are interested, we'll trade you a case of the Napoleon brandy for two hundred gallons of your jet fuel. That should see us through the next thousand years."

"A deal!" they shouted all together.

"Fine. The brandy is already aboard, and we have removed the fuel. Now good-bye, we have had about all of your primitive presences that we can stand."

They waved cheery good-byes and tramped back into the *Pleasantville Eagle*, passing the bottle happily from hand to hand. A hoarse Sally emerged from the head, and they gave her a double slug to help her throat. Three had not lied, since he was incapable of it, and there on a seat

153

in the front row was a case of the brandy, while in the seat next to it was a golden sphere about the size of a golfball with a single red button on it labeled "press me."

"These roaches sure know a thing or two about microminiaturization," John said, slipping the sphere into his pocket. "Now how do we get out of here?"

"Maximum power, I would say," Chuck said. "We can make it almost back to Haggis in a single jump. In that way the warring thousands around this sphere will have no idea that we were ever inside."

"I'll buy that," John said. "Maximum power, lady and gents, so hold onto your hats."

Jerry twisted the dials to their stops, made careful alignment, then pressed the actuator button. This was the biggest jump they had ever made, and they really felt it. As if their guts were made of spaghetti and were being wound up on a big fork.

"Yukh," Sally eructated when they had emerged light-years away, speaking for them all, then staggered and sat down heavily in a seat.

It took them awhile to recover from the shock of the jump—the Napoleon brandy helped a good deal—and when they finally landed at the Galaxy Ranger base on Planet X, they were feeling better, as well as being half crocked, so Sally brewed some black coffee and they all drank a good deal of this before they emerged and marched grimly to the control room.

"Report!" John said, seating himself at the massive control console and flipping switches quickly. Most of the switches didn't work, since they were still building the place, but he finally got through to the OD.

"Glad you are back, sir," the alien said. "That spy team you sent to track the Lortonoi is back and, boy, do they have a story to tell!"

"All right, don't ruin the punch line, just send the commander in here on the double."

The commander turned out to be Pipa, his green skin now taut and smooth since he was eating better, his familiar grin splitting his wide head from earslit to earslit.

"Hi, Jerry," he croaked. "Long time no see, not since

154

the dustup in the DnDrf mine. Those were the good old days—"

"Look!" John ordered. "Report first, reminisce later if you don't mind. You tracked the fleeing Lortonoi?"

"That we did, sir, like the hound of hell, tracking them as they fled down through the light-years. Their track ended in a star cluster out on the galactic rim, or rather at one star in particular that is called Diesun. This star has a rather unusual planet or satellite or whatever the hell you want to call it. Sorry, chief, but my powers of description fail me. Let me flash a slide on the screen, and then I'll fill in the details. You're not going to believe this, I know we didn't. Could I have the first slide, please?"

A solidograph picture instantly appeared in midair before them, and they gasped in unison.

"I don't believe it," John said. "What kind of funny games you up to, you miserable toad?"

"Please, have patience, I beg! I can get the rest of the crew in, and we'll swear loyalty and truth on bended knee and take a polygraph test, the works. *This* is what we found out there."

This was a thing like a hula hoop in space. It could have been a discarded hunk of machinery or something like that until you looked at the *scale*. For that sphere of light floating in its center was a sun. Or rather a *sun*. This whatchmacallit in space was floating, rotating, around the sun like an immense wheel without spokes.

"I know what they've done," Jerry said, snapping his fingers loudly. "It was in the astronomical literature a couple of years back, a real mad idea. But this proves that no idea is so mad that there isn't someone—or something—somewhere just mad enough to try it."

"Would you kindly tell us just what the hell you are talking about?" John snapped.

"Happily. Here is what you do if you have unlimited energy and plenty of time. Say you got a solar system like our own solar system. You've been mining the habitable planets, namely, Earth, for a long time, drilling wells and that kind of thing. So what happens? You know what happens. You start running out. The wells run dry, the miner-

155

als are all used up, and things begin to look poorly. Of course you can send spaceships to other planets to open mines, but there is a problem in logistics and getting the stuff back and so forth. So what you do, if you are set up for it, and somebody really was if we can believe this slide, you rearrange the whole solar system. You bash all the planets and moons together, which melts them up, and then you extrude this molten gunk through a large orifice until you get a long tube of the stuff, and then you flatten the tube so you have like a long plank or maybe a ribbon in space. After that, all you have to do is join the ends of the ribbon together so they stick and you got a big hoop which rotates around the sun."

"What have you been drinking—or smoking?" John asked suspiciously.

"Come on! You asked for the theory, so I'm giving it to you. I'm not telling you *how* to do it, just what to do. So, you have this hula hoop floating around the sun, and after a while it cools down so you can land on it and plant trees and bring the people and the animals and such back and you have a real nifty world. You build the thing at the correct distance from the sun so the temperature is just right, and all the time the same since there is no night and day since the thing doesn't rotate but spins instead. You've also arranged so that all the minerals are easily available and can be dug up by strip mining. What resources you have! A planet like Jupiter has maybe a million times as much minerals as poor old Earth. So with plenty of raw materials, sunshine, peace, and prosperity you can throw away the birth control pills and just let the population grow. This hula hoop world will have like a billion times the surface available for population, so it will be a long time before you fill it up. All in all it may sound like a nutty idea, but if you can get it to work, you have a good deal going."

"Or the Lortonoi have a good deal going," John mused, looking at the slide, and a sudden chill passed over them all.

What mischief those monsters could create if they controlled a hoop world like this one! The same black thought

156

possessed them all at the same time, and an aura of gloom obsessed the room. It was John who finally broke the dark silence, and there was a cheery note to his words.

"Cheer up, guys! It's always darkest before the dawn!"

"Piss off, you pollyannaish sod," Jerry muttered, wishing they had thought to bring the brandy with them.

"I mean it. Aren't we forgetting this?" He took the tiny golden sphere from his shirt pocket and tossed it, glinting, into the air. "Things *have* to get worse before they can get better. So let us hope that the Lortonoi are really up to some loathsome piece of nastiness out there, something so awful that we can report to the Chachkas and get Krakar to polish them off once and for all. I hate to sound like a warmonger, but the worse things get now, the better they will be in the long run."

Jerry laughed aloud. "You're right, you know. So let's fire up our entire fleet of battle cruisers and space battleships and go out there and see if we can cause some real trouble!"

18

THE MIGHTIEST ARMADA
—LAUNCHED!

It was a mighty armada of space the likes of which had never been seen before in the lenticular galaxy, or in the nearby spiral galaxy, or in any galaxy for that matter. Representatives of a thousand races were here, sentient creatures who were physically different in every way; rocklike Felsenig from the ten gravity world of Felsen, fairylike Guntzel-pogue from the tenth gravity world of the same name, snakelike Slangeorm, vegetablelike Karotene, sluglike Caracoller—and thousands more. If you were to put them in the same room together—it would have to be a rather large, air-conditioned room—it really would be a kind of loathsome sight. But what is beauty except in the eye of the beholder, and some of these things, aliens rather, didn't even have eyes. But they had loved ones and mates, sometimes up to sixteen when there were that many sexes, as with the Jigajig, who did almost nothing except that because it was so complicated. They knew the heights of elation, the depths of despair. They were free. Well, most of them were. And the despots were usually kind despots. But what mattered was that each one of these free races were living their lives in the way they wanted and were not being ruled by outsiders. They had joined together under the banner of freedom to fight against the loathsome Lortonoi, who would have ruled and crushed them all.

At the heart of the immense fleet was the former space armada of the Hagg-Loos, donated by the Hagg-Inder, who had won the final battle and instantly stripped their insane relatives of all capacity to wage further war. Stretching out on both sides, and back into the distance as far as the eye could see, were the spacers of all the other races. Here they were, the volunteers from worlds who had known the terror of the Lortonoi and would do anything to fight that galactic menace, spaceships from free worlds that knew you could not subdivide liberty and were willing to fight for that cause, great thundering spacers from other free worlds who wanted to stay free and "voluntarily" donated a few spacers to the fleet when it hovered above their planets. They were all here—and what a heterogeneous sight it was! Mile-long gray metal battleships, fast, needlepointed scouts, great lumbering gunships made of small planetoids on which giant space cannon had been mounted.

While, there, up front, leading this tremendous fleet, was the silver form of the *Pleasantville Eagle*! Old Glory had been painted proudly on both sides of her immense tail, with the United Nations flag much smaller down below. Wings spread like the eagle she was, she stayed there in the van. Beware, Lortonoi, because the Galaxy Rangers are on the prowl. Shake with fear in your dank dens though you may, justice is coming closer, light-year by light-year, with every passing moment.

A banquet had been spread in the lounge of the old *Eagle*. Whiter than white tablecloths and sparkling silver drew the eye, while the nose twitched with appreciation at the succulent smells emerging from the kitchen. The top echelon of the Galaxy Rangers gathered for a last celebration before the space armada reached the star Diesun and its strange satellite. John, as Ranger Number One was at the head of the table, with the other Earthmen on each side of him. Sally would, they hoped, join them later; meanwhile, she was sweating it out in the galley with her assistants. The other Rangers crowded the tables, shoulder to shoulder, drinking and laughing together irrespective of the color of their skins; black, red, white, green, polkadot, all mingled and drank. Except, of course, for Lord Prrsi and the other red-hot races who had a heated corner to themselves. Loud laughter rose, hearty shouts, and an occasional belch. This was comradeship indeed, the likes of which had never been seen before. After they had dined

159

and Sally had showered and joined them, John tapped on his wineglass for attention, and an expectant hush fell.

"Rangers, our moment of destiny is upon us. Our agents throughout the lenticular galaxy report no activity by the Lortonoi. We have driven them from refuge to refuge until now they have reached the end of their rope and have holed up upon the strange construction circling the nearby sun, Diesun. They are trapped! And we are upon them. There will be a battle, and there will be bloodshed, but it will all be in a noble cause. To destroy the Lortonoi is worth any sacrifice. . . ."

"*Ooooooonnnnh. . . .*"

This ghastly sound broke through his words and silenced him, a keening wail of agony from the centermost table. A chair fell over, and a plump green figure writhed on the rug.

"Aid for that Ranger!" John ordered. "He has been taken ill."

"Don't touch him!" another green alien, not unlike the first, cried out, jumping to his feet. "Pipa and I are of the same race, from the planet Bachtria, and I recognize the symptoms. Our race is an ancient one, and we are possessed of psionic abilities like no other. Normally these psi powers lie dormant, but occasionally, in periods of immense stress, when something strange looms in the future and coming events cast their shadows before them, why, then those sensitives of our race manage to break through the temporal barrier. This is happening at this moment to my colleague, Pipa, now writhing there upon your rug. His body is now only a shell while his *ego* moves into the future. Soon it will return with a message, and you must all be silent and listen. I know not what that message will be, but I do know that it will be a matter of grave importance, of life and death, for at no other times is the psi-*ego* torn from the body in this manner. Hark! He begins to speak."

"Korax . . . korax . . ." Pipa croaked, then mumbled more words incoherently. The tension strained and tightened, and there was scarcely a breath drawn as the words became clearer, comprehensible to them all.

"Woe! Oh, woe! What ghastliness lies ahead . . . all

things are not as they seem . . . victory is defeat and winners shall lose . . . woe, woe. Take heed, for a trap is being set and the end of the galaxy as we know it is at hand . . . many gathered here today will never meet again. Now mark me . . . and mark me well . . . say your good-byes, for the end is near!"

After this the voice became incoherent again and degenerated to a mumble, and the mumble turned into a snore as Pipa slept soundly upon the floor.

"And exactly what does all that mean?" John asked the other Bachtrian, who shrugged his green shoulders in despair.

"Beats me, Number One. These *ego* trips tend to speak in riddles and that kind of thing, so it is anybody's guess. But he did seem to be sort of clear there toward the end, and if you don't mind, let me say good-bye to you now and shake your hand. It sure has been great up to now to be a Ranger, and if you have to die, it is best to die in a worthy cause. I think. Though of course I would really prefer not to die at all."

With these words he hopped over to John and pumped his hand. After this there was a lot of solemn good-bye saying and hand shaking, and the party broke up under a cloud of gloom.

"Well, I must say," Sally declared. "After all that cooking and trouble, it certainly appears that it really wasn't worth it."

"That was great friend Ormoloo," John told her, attempting to insert a note of cheer, but it did no good. In a minute the Earthlings were alone again, surrounded by the debris of the deserted banquet.

"I'll wash if you'll dry," Chuck said.

"Not now," Jerry snapped. "There are more important things to consider. Just shovel everything into a big box, and we'll worry about it later. In just a matter of hours we will be popping out of the space warp near this damn hula hoop in space, and from what our green friend predicted it is not going to be a pushover. Anyone got any ideas?"

"We'll have to go in first," Chuck said. "We have the only cheddite projector mounted on this ship, so we can

161

get into and out of trouble faster than anything else in the fleet. Why don't we have them hold just one space warp away so they can come arunnin' when we blow the whistle? Meanwhile, we go in quick, get the lay of the land, and split if it gets too hot."

"I agree," John agreed. "It's dangerous, but it's the only chance we have of finding out a thing before the entire fleet is committed. I vote let's go."

"I'm with you," Jerry said.

"You're all insane!" Sally cried. "It is suicide. Let someone else do it."

They smiled wry smiles at her, and John spoke for them all.

"Sorry, Sally, old girl, but we can't oblige. The chip is on the Lortonoi shoulder, and we are just going to have to knock it off. Why do men fight bulls? Race high-speed cars? Go to the Moon? Climb Mount Everest? Because they are there—"

"Nuts! You do it for the old *machismo*, bragging about who has the biggest *cojones*. Well, I'll have nothing to do with it. I'm going to clean up this mess and then go to bed with a sleeping pill and a murder mystery and hope that I wake up alive, not dead."

They laughed when she left, knowing she was just a simple hysterical woman, then turned themselves to men's destructive work. Orders were issued to the fleet, which slowly ground to a halt, with a few fatal crashes, of course, which is to be expected when you try to stop a fleet of thousands of giant spaceships. The Rangers who manned the battle stations aboard the *Pleasantville Eagle* were all in position, and Lord Prrsi poked his head up from the hatch to the insulated hold to see the action. One by one the green lights blinked on on the ready board, signifying that every position was manned and ready, until the entire board was green, except for the red light from Sally's compartment, where she was zonked out by two Seconals washed down with twenty cc. of Noctec.

"Are you ready, Rangers?" John called out, and from every compartment, except one of course, came back the echoing shout. "Then here we go!"

162

In a single slithering jump the great airplane-spaceship plunged through into the lambda dimension and popped out again not far from the bright star Diesun. Every alarm went off and they stared at the visiplates at a great battle in space going on not too far from them. Fantastically powerful battleships—the smallest of them would dwarf the largest they had in their fleet—were locked in dogged conflict. They used energy weapons with great prolificacy, and all space was filled with the shock and shimmer of the ravening forces that tore at the very fabric of space itself. Ravening rays worried at the force screens that shielded other ships, while force fields of highly charged ions, no more than a few feet in diameter but having the power of a hundred hydrogen bombs, floated about ready to explode at the slightest touch. John touched the controls and pulled the ship back a few thousand miles, and they all nodded agreement.

"Easier to watch on the long-distance scope," Jerry said offhandedly. "We don't want to really mix with them until we learn the score."

"We don't want to mix with them at *all*," John said, speaking aloud what they all were thinking. "I've got a feeling we are kind of playing out of our league with these babies."

"Cheer up," Jerry said, pointing at the screen. "Don't forget there are two sides there, and they seem pretty even. One of them has to be on our side—I hope—so it's not as bad as it looks. I think."

"ATTENTION!" Alarms buzzed again, and the radar operator's voice cut in above them. "Object approaching on collision course from the direction of space battle. Estimated ETA, fourteen seconds."

"Strap in! Am taking evasion measures," Jerry said into the intercom. "Here we go!"

They darted away at right angles and hovered expectantly, every screen focused on the oncoming danger. Was it a space battleship on their tail? Or perhaps a missile? Time would tell. And it did.

"A piece of wreckage," Chuck said. "Looks like a big chunk torn out of one of the spacers that blew up."

"I'll match velocities," Jerry announced, fingers busy at the controls. "This may answer some questions, if there is still anyone alive in that hunk of junk. Mind shields on, everyone, just in case there are Lortonoi aboard or in mental control. And, Chuck, be a good fellow and slip down and put Sally's on her, just for a change, and for God's sake, tie it into place this time."

Nearer and nearer the chunk of spatial debris came, until they could see that it was a slice cut out of a battle ship by ravening rays, sort of like a Tum pulled out of the package, a disk, you know. All the compartments they could see were filled with incomprehensible machinery, now gutted and burned out and empty.

"Looks pretty bad," Jerry mused. "I'll try the radio, just in case." He flicked switches rapidly and spoke into the microphone. "Hello, hunk of space debris formerly part of a great battleship. Do you read me? We are close by and offer help. Over."

The speaker fried and burbled with the static of distant stars, but otherwise all was silent.

"Try 176.45 kilocycles," John suggested. "That is the emergency band a lot of spaceships use. These people may know it too."

Jerry repeated his message on this frequency, and this time, when he threw the switches, a distant hissing could be heard and a weak voice.

"Can read you. Oxygen almost gone. Open space lock so I can board. Sole survivor."

"Jump to it, guys!" John ordered and the smooth-working team functioned as if it were running on oiled ball bearings. The magnet ray operators drew the clumsy piece of junk close while the cargo operator opened the outer hatch. A moment later there was a thump and a bump as *something* entered the lock, and the outer hatch closed. Mighty pumps throbbed as they pushed air back into the lock chamber, and when the pressure had been equalized, the inner door opened automatically, and every eye was upon it. What would the alien possessor of the weak voice look like?

He looked a lot different from anything their wildest

164

speculations could have imagined. Bending, to get through the opening, came an individual who stood at least eight feet tall from the top of his head crest to the bottom of his clawed feet. And he was impressive! Just as mankind enjoys a sort of simian ancestry, primates and all that, and the Bachtrians emerged from the swamps in froggy form, so did this strange individual obviously have a certain animal phylum or species in his background. Birds! And what a bird he was! His immense yellow beak would tear open a boiler plate as easily as an aluminum beer can. His eyes were piercing and hooded, like a great hawk or eagle. He wore no clothes, nor did he need any, for his magnificent plumage was clothing enough. His large wings were folded on his back, and the claws on his three immense toes tore gaping rents in the carpet as he walked. Unlike most birds, however, he had two well-built arms, as well as wings, and he hooked his well-built thumbs into his wide gunbelt as he strode into their midst and stopped.

"Who is master here?" he asked with the air of one who commands.

"I am Galaxy Ranger Number One," John said, striding over fearlessly to stand before the giant figure. "Men call me John."

"Greetings, John. I am Troceps of the Fligigleh and am called that only by my friends. You have saved my life, therefore, I owe you a life. Whom shall I kill?" His fingers twitched at his gun butt.

"Hold on, Troceps, old chicken, we don't hold with that sort of thing. Thanks will do, and the slate is wiped clean."

"I say thanks and *your* slate is wiped clean, John old ape, but *mine* is not. If I can kill no one for you, why, then I must kill myself."

His gun leaped from the holster, and he poked it against one staring eye while John leaned forward to restrain him.

"No need for that sort of thing here. Get feathers and blood all over the place. Wait a bit and we'll get you a prisoner or a spy to knock off. . . ."

"Spy, now that is a good idea." He glared around the room with hawklike stare, and all there swayed away from

165

that merciless glance. "Ah, yes, there is always one, count on that. A weak creature, ex-slave, who has sold out to his decadent master on his miserable home planet who reports directly to the loathsome Lortonoi. He is filled with fear now, but he is not sure it is he I am talking about. I laugh in his beak, I mean teeth! He knows not the penetrating power of my thoughts, thought power that is even stronger than the Lortonoi. Therefore, I give him a clue so he will know I know he knows I know. The clue is this—your mother's maiden name is *Ixstaiclj!*"

The krung-field operator jumped up from his station and whipped out his gun, but fast as he was, Troceps was the faster. A single bolt of energy sped from his blaster, and the hapless spy was instant charcoal.

"The debt is paid, and we are even," Troceps proclaimed, blowing into the muzzle of his blaster, then coughing at the smoke that eddied out around his head.

"Well done," John said. "Now, with ceremonies out of the way, could you tell us who you are, what your outfit is, what is going on out there in that space battle, where you come from, that sort of thing? Just so we can get to know you better. And what was that name you mentioned, sounded like Lortonoi? Who are they—friends of yours?"

He smiled cheerfully as he talked and casually loosened his gun in his holster while a whispering sound slithered through the cabin as everyone else loosened their guns in their holsters. There was tension in the air, while all eyes were on the newcomer. Troceps shook his great wings, and a feather came loose. He caught it before it touched the floor and used it to pick his beak with. The silence and tension stretched—and broke suddenly as Troceps put his head back and roared with laughter.

"I should not laugh," he said, laughing and wiping the tears from his eyes with a touch of the feather. "But you are all so transparent. After my demonstration you must realize that I can penetrate the simple mind shield you wear and know your every thought. So you will know mine too, I invite you, the hot one over there with his head sticking out of the floor, to enter my brain and read

166

my innermost thoughts. I see you have great powers of mental strength. Enter—my mind is an open book!"

"Happy to oblige," Lord Prrsi said and clacked his claws in concentration. It took only a matter of moments for him to get in and get out, and his claws clacked the louder. "I say, chaps," he enthused. "This blighter is one of us. His people have been fighting the Lortonoi for simply ages!"

19

LOATHSOME LORTONOI
UNVEILED!

Enthusiastic shouts of joy echoed from the cabin walls at
the realization that there were new recruits to the banner
of the anti-Lortonoi forces. And what recruits! Fighting
men like Troceps here, as well as incredible space battleships such as the ones they had seen locked in combat.

"Locked in combat," John thought. "Just a second,
Troceps, old parrot. Glad to have you on our side and all
that, but *who* were the guys you were fighting out there?
Not to run down your space armada or anything, but you
seemed to be pretty well matched with the nasties. Would
you care to fill us in?"

"Happy to. But first—do you have a bowl of water?"

"We have a bowl of anything you want, including
hundred-year-old brandy."

"The water will do fine. It is not for me; we Fligigleh
have rugged constitutions and can fight for weeks on a
handful of birdseed. The water is for my little pet,
Pishky."

As he said this, he held up his blaster and unscrewed
the base of the butt which proved to be hollow, and from
its interior there dropped a little green turtle that scrab-
bled about in the palm of his hand.

"Looks just like a little green turtle from Earth," Jerry
said, speaking for all of them.

"Very possibly. But as I see in your minds, you Earthlings keep birds for pets, and that is just the way we Fligigleh keep turtles. They are considered good-luck charms,
and whenever I go into battle, little Pishky rides along
happy in my gun butt—"

"Look, not to interrupt," John interrupted, "but can't

we do the turtle thing later? We would rather hear about that other fleet and stuff."

"But of course, I will explain." But he didn't until the water appeared, and little Pishky was paddling about with turtle eyes staring up stupidly at the happy face of its aquiline master. Troceps stroked its shell with his forefinger before turning his attention back to his hosts. "It is a story that goes back a long way, but the entire story must be told for you to grasp any single part of it. My race is an ancient one, so ancient that by any of your standards of measurement you cannot measure the amount of time we have been around. Since earliest time we were bothered with production problems and population problems. There are two things we really like to do, and they are build bigger and better machines and lay plenty of eggs. Ahh, the sight of those eggs! But I digress. Any male Fligigleh considers himself a failure and blows his brains out if he doesn't have at least twenty chicks and a personal car at least thirty meters long. Well, I see that you begin to get the problem. We invented a space drive, moved on and occupied all the nearest worlds and so forth, but we aren't really the space-conquering types. All we want to do is stay home and lay eggs and drive around in our forty-meter-long cars. So some unsung genius cooked up this idea of mashing together all the planets in a star system until they melted, then stretching them out into a belt and sending the whole thing spinning around. This was done, and we left all our occupied worlds and settled on this new world, which is named Cotorra after the inventor of the technique, so maybe he is not so unsung either. Ahh, look at little Pishky scratch his weensie claws against the glass, scrabbling with wide-eyed stupidity!"

"Nice turtle, sure," Chuck said, smiling falsely. "But could you sort of tell us what happened next after you all settled down on Cotorra?"

"Be patient, I said it would be long in the telling. We settled down and enjoyed our way of life. Uncontrolled breeding and car building, and there was no end in sight for millions of years. More space was available for nests and roads as we expanded out from the original site of settlement. And this did go on for millions of years, pure bliss I assure you, a period in our history we always refer to as the Golden Egg Years, but it was to come to an end. The Lortonoi arrived!"

Troceps squawked the name out with great irritation, lashing out his foot unconsciously at the same time so that his great claws ripped a seat to pieces and tore gaping rents in the carpet and the dural floor beneath.

"Oh, those evil Lortonoi! Although we have excellent powers of the mind, some genealogical change had occurred in our race as it spread in both directions out from the original site. By this time we had occupied almost three-quarters of the hoop that is our world, and in a few million more years the expanding frontiers would have met and we would have to think about maybe making another world like this or perhaps patching in an extra piece or something. But this was fated never to occur. The Lortonoi discovered that a crunched gene or something had so weakened the mental strength of the Fligigleh at the left end of the expansion that their minds could be entered and controlled by the Lortonoi. We on the right still maintained our traditional mental health and expelled their slimy thoughts the second they touched our pristine brains. I am sure that you see the setup now. The leftists began arming, and we armed too in self-defense. At first a ground war occupied the opposing forces and the space between the expanding population fronts became a no-man's-land. However, as weapons became more powerful, this proved impractical since our hoop isn't that thick and it could have been blown right through, which wouldn't help anybody. So air war began, then space war as both sides sought to protect their populations, and the whole thing expanded farther and farther into space along this front. So, for millennia now, we have been locked in this endless war, which serves to keep our population down and our factories humming. We both draw supplies and soldiers from our rear and build bigger and better war machines until the result, as you would have seen if you watched the battle during which my ship was destroyed, is space war on a scale never considered before. I must add,

170

in closing, that the recent engagement was only the most minor clash between very weak scout ship patrols and of no importance. You should see what happens when the really *big* battleships mix it up."

A shudder ran through the room at this news, and John had to swallow heavily before he could speak.

"Well, I guess it is good for you that we are here to throw our armed might into the conflict on your side, tip the balance that will win the war for liberty."

"I don't mean to scoff," Troceps said in a very superior manner. "But I have examined the size of your fleet through your memories and, not meaning to be insulting, old primate, your forces wouldn't stand the chance of a snowball in hell up against the enemy. Zap! They would be cinders in microseconds."

"Well, I'm not sure of that," John said defensively. "And it is not only the fleet which is so great, but we have the cheddite projector which can whisk their battleships into the sun before they get close enough to fire." He picked up the cheddite projector, which still looked like a five-cell flashlight, and waved it proudly as all the others cheered.

"Oh, that," Troceps said, and of course his beak showed no expression, but if it *could* have showed expression, it certainly would have shown a sneer. "We know all about that already. It seems the Lortonoi appeared with one of those things awhile back, and they did manage to pick off a battleship or two before our scientists developed a kappa radiation screen that completely stops the radiation from the thing, and that is that. But it is nice of you to offer, and we do appreciate it, but my suggestion is that you all split before you get squashed by the big boys. Maybe we can't lick the Lortonoi, but we sure have them stopped—and have had them stopped for a long time. The only thing we have not been able to do is crack the mind screen that covers their headquarters, so we have no idea of what they look like. Other than that we have things under control and will hold the forefront of this battle against the common enemy. You can go home."

"No we can't," Jerry pouted, sulking for all of them.

"The Galaxy Rangers were organized to wipe out the Lortonoi, and we cannot stop until that is done. Nothing else is possible."

"One thing is," Jerry said, in a strange voice. "The Galaxy Rangers could be wiped out instead."

"Bite your tongue!" Chuck shouted. "What's got into you that you should be talking like that?"

Jerry chuckled evilly, and his tongue flashed in and out like a serpent's, and his voice dripped venom when he spoke. "That's just about the size of it. What's got into me. . . ."

"He is possessed by a Lortonoi!" Lord Prrsi shouted. "I can detect the alien presence stronger than I have ever detected it before."

"Yes, the Lortonoi are here, and it is the end of the ballgame for you libertarian, religious swine. We are taking over. We have won!"

"What do you mean?" Chuck gasped, inadvertently stepping back from his occupied friend.

"I mean that this is the moment we set the stage for. We wanted all the forces opposed to us to be gathered together at the same time so we could destroy them. They are here now and will be destroyed by the Fligigleh forces we command."

"You forget about the Fligigleh forces you don't command," crowed Troceps, striding forward. "I hope you people won't mind, but I am afraid I will have to open up your friend like a sausage with one blow of my clawed heel. This Lortonoi must go."

"Stop!" Lortonoi-Jerry commanded, and very much to his own surprise, Troceps stopped. "Now, at last, the truth can be revealed. We can control *any* Fligigleh mind. We just said we couldn't in order to get this great big war going. We arranged that both sides would be so evenly matched that they couldn't destroy each other so that they would have to build bigger and better fleets. They have done this and put together these two fleets. Supplied by the unlimited resources of Cotorra, they are unstoppable and unbeatable. And now the fleets *will* be combined. Everything has been planned from the beginning. There was

172

one little hitch there when the Earthling appeared with the cheddite projector, but we took care of that as you see. We stole a projector and used it in battle so that the Fligigleh scientist could come up with a defense. We've done it, we've got it made, the galaxy is ours, we cannot be stopped and . . . STOP!"

He bellowed this last at John who had taken the golden sphere out of his shirt pocket and was about to press the button.

"I was waiting for that," Jerry-Lortonoi sneered. "This was the one weapon we were afraid of. Krakar. Now we know all about it, ha-ha. So, go ahead and press the button!"

But, strain as he might, John could not. His finger was only a fraction of an inch above the *press me* button—but it would not descend. His body shook with the effort as he strained with every fiber of his being to push that finger down—but it would not! The Lortonoi brain was the stronger, and that evil creature was just toying with him, for it had absolute control. Struggle was useless. Chuck jumped to help him, but long before that help could arrive John watched, horrified, as his hand opened and the golden sphere dropped to the floor.

Where the heel of his boot slowly ground it into gleaming fragments.

Grinding all their hopes along with it.

"I said it was our ball game!" Jerry sneered victoriously. "So, at last, in this moment of supreme triumph, we can at last reveal our presence and our real identity. I am here, among you, the Lortonoi you have been seeking. Do you not see me?"

There was a shuffle throughout the ship as Ranger drew back from Ranger, eyeing each other with suspicion, fingering their weapons. Lord Prrsi eyed along with the others, and he used his immense mental powers as well.

"It is here," he muttered. "I can sense that, but my mind is clouded by its presence, for the Lortonoi mental powers are beyond all others. Yet I swear I cannot find the enemy although I have scanned the minds of all here."

"All?" Jerry asked. "Not quite all."

173

"Yoo-hoo!" A powerful thought blasted through every mind at once. "I see *you!*"

Now their eyes were drawn across the room and down. Down toward the table. Down toward the bowl of water. Down to the little green turtle that was waving its tiny claws at them.

"Pishky . . . *you!*" Troceps gasped.

"Lord Pishky, if you don't mind. Member of the Lortonoi Council of ten, now rulers of the galaxy. How we fooled you—and how we hate you! You, you great lumbering creatures with fingers and hands and tentacles and that kind of thing. While we, with the greatest brains the galaxy had ever seen, are trapped in these tiny worthless bodies. How we *loathe* you! We have tried to breed for size and such, but whenever we do, like the turtles we planted on Earth, size brings with it mindless stupidity, so that experiment has stopped. We decided instead to use our powers to enslave and destroy you all, and at last, after millennia of effort, the day of conquest is at hand. The Lortonoi have won!"

After the first numbed surprise every creature in the ship surged forward, each fighting for the chance to get the Lortonoi under his heel. But their efforts were doomed. For, still laughing, the tiny green turtle gripped their minds and threw them back. It was defeat indeed.

"I don't want to die! I'm getting out of here!" John gasped, and turning the cheddite projector on himself, he vanished.

"The first rat leaves the sinking spaceship," Lord Pishky sneered, which is very hard to do if you are a turtle. "He has gone back to the fleet, but since the fleet is due to be destroyed in a few microseconds, it will do him no good. Already we Lortonoi are taking over the opposing Fligigleh space fleets and making them one. How we have laughed at you from our security as your pets! We controlled your thoughts so that you liked us and kept us around, preparing yourselves for the moment of your destruction. Now the end is at hand, the fleet approaches, so if any of you want to have a last prayer—I won't allow it!

174

Ha-ha! How we hate you God freaks. Prepare yourself, for the end is at hand."

"Oh, no, it's not," John said, appearing suddenly in the middle of the cabin. He was dressed in a spacesuit and was carrying a sack over one shoulder. "You'll never get away with this conquest, not while I have this!"

He reached into the sack and withdrew a long, red, succulent shape and waved it over his head.

It was a kosher garlic salami!

20

THE SECRET OF
THE SALAMI

"Are you out of your mind?" Jerry gasped, speaking for all of them, free to speak for himself again now that the Lortonoi no longer needed him for a mouthpiece.

"Not as mad as you think, Jerry, my boy. When you all tried to attack Pishky, the mad little green turtle Lortonoi, awhile back there, I had the glimmerings of an idea deep down. I acted instantly before Pishky could read my mind and while it was still mostly involved in holding you all off. I suppressed the thought and instead felt immense fear, which, you will understand, was not hard to do. Then I thought of escape, fleeing to the fleet, grabbing a ship and running, yes, I would do that! I turned the cheddite projector on myself, and the Lortonoi, fooled for the moment, let me go. But once back in the fleet, I abandoned all thoughts of flight and set about my *real* task. I got into a spacesuit and used the cheddite projector to go back to the space battle around the Chachka golden sphere. I almost didn't make it, the battle is raging worse than ever, but I managed to align the projector precisely and made it inside the dome in one jump. After that the rest is obvious. The Chachkas read my mind, discovered what had happened, and upon the instant decided that the time had come at last, after all the millennia, to use Krakar." He waved the salami again. "And Krakar is here, within the salami, which is a disguise."

"Well, it will never be used." Pishky radiated the powerful thought, and instantly everyone in the ship was frozen. "Except perhaps by us. Now—hand over that salami, and you, get a knife and let us see what this device looks like."

But no one moved, despite the waves of thought that

radiated out from the bowl where the green turtle-Lortonoi swam around distractedly. There was a stir from the sack still suspended from John's shoulder and up out of it crawled a familiar, black, cockroach-shaped form that stopped on his shoulder and stared down at the bowl.

"It is Three of the Chachkas!" Chuck shouted. "We are saved!"

"Yes, you are saved," the creature said, "but no, I am not Three but Four. Three was busy. But I can handle this job myself. Know this, oh, vile Lortonoi, we have been watching your evil race for millennia. Rather we weren't watching you, even our magnificent minds could not penetrate the mind barrier erected around your secret headquarters, but we were watching what you were doing and didn't like it at all. A long time ago we decided that if Krakar were ever used, it would be used against you swine, and our decision has proved correct. Now you have exposed your real identity so we can wage war upon you and destroy you down to the last fragment of shell . . ."

Four's words were interrupted by a bolt of mental energy hurled at it by the creature in the bowl. So great was this thrust that every mind in the ship blacked out for an instant, and all the lights went out as well. Then the emergency lights came on, and they gasped as they saw the burned hole in the carpet where the strength of Four's brain had deflected the bolt.

"That was your turn," Four said calmly. "Now it is mine."

With these words they were locked in silent, mental conflict, giant brain against giant brain. There was a tension in the air that they all sensed, for this was the battle to determine the fate of the galaxy. Who would win? The creatures, fighting turtle, gallant cockroach, seemed equally matched as the seconds, then minutes, flew by and there was no change.

But was there? Why was Pishky swimming around the bowl in that agitated manner and trying to climb up the glass sides? Was that a tiny streamer of vapor rising from the water.

"Great Cacodyl," Lord Prrsi choked out. "The Chachka

is holding his own in the mental battle, I can detect that, but so mighty is its brain that it is diverting part of its mental energy to heat up the water in the bowl so that it is rapidly approaching the boiling point!"

They watched in frozen silence as the tiny, yet extremely evil creature paddled about furiously as the water began to bubble. The end was not long in coming. There was a mental cry of despair that swept through their minds and then was gone—and with it went that evil presence that had sought to destroy them all.

"We've won," Jerry said, stepping forward slowly and picking up the bowl. "Not only that, but we have some turtle soup."

"If you wanted some sandwiches, though how you could after that big banquet," Sally said, coming into the room, "why didn't you wake me and tell me? You know the kind of mess you always make. You want the salami on rye?" she asked, plucking the elongated form from John's fingers and putting it on the cutting board and raising a knife.

"Stop!" a number of voices cried at one time, and stop she did, since every mind capable of mind control was now fighting to control hers and to stop the knife from ascending. She bounced and jiggled, and the knife dropped from her fingers, and John bent and picked up the salami carefully.

"In my hands," he intoned, "I hold the fate of the known universe."

"I thought it was a kosher salami," Sally said, but no one was listening.

With infinite care, under Four's mental instructions, he removed the skin and carefully made a long slice into the meat. Then, slowly and carefully, he reached into the opening and took out Krakar.

"If you hadn't told me, I wouldn't have believed it!" Jerry said, his jaw dropping loosely.

"Me neither!" Chuck agreed.

"It looks like a spray can of oven cleaner," Sally said, unimpressed.

178

"Its physical shape does not matter," Four said in no uncertain terms. "For this is *Krakar!*"

"Could you tell us how it works—and quickly?" John said, eyeing the subspatial radar. "Because the combined fleets of the Fligigleh are now coming this way at full blast."

"I cannot possibly explain to your childish minds how the device works, though of course there is a wiring diagram painted on the can. But I can tell you how to operate it and what it does. You hold it on one hand and point the orifice at the enemy and press the plastic button on top."

"I told you, just like stove cleaner spray," Sally said, but was glared into silence by the others and left the cabin, miffed.

"What Krakar is is a temporal catalyst that unites its target with the time flow that sweeps through the universe. But it unites it *backward* to the normal flow so that a blockade is set up. Well, as you know, *nothing* can stand against the time flow so the blockade instantly becomes a temporal tornado that whirls faster and faster and sucks in all matter for a couple of light-years in every direction as it gathers speed; then, when it hits top revolutions, it *blasts* through the fabric of time itself and hurtles in reverse for approximately thirty-one trillion years. . . ."

"The figure is exact?" Chuck asked.

"Of course."

"Big bang?"

"Obviously, and I am pleased that at least one *entity* here knows what the hell I am talking about. I can see by your bulging eyes and hanging jaws that I had better supply a little more detail. Not only must Krakar be used against a mortal enemy of the galaxy, but it *must* be used, and at that only used once. So you see why we were so careful about it. Because the fleet of ships hurled into the past will pick up temporal energy on the way, and when it emerges at that early date it will explode with a *really* big bang and that will be the birth of the universe. I'll leave you to ponder on the philosophical permutations of that for a bit while I install this mind screen." He dived back into the bag that John was still holding and emerged with a black sphere from which sprang a length of cord and a two pronged plug. "You got a hundred-and-ten-volt outlet here?"

John pointed it out, then climbed out of his spacesuit to help him plug it in. The Chachka made delicate adjustments on the device, then threw a switch.

"It is working," he said. "Now the Lortonoi will not be able to control the mind of anyone in this ship no matter how hard they try."

"What difference does that make?" Jerry asked. "Since they'll be sucked into the temporal tornado in a couple of minutes."

"I will explain. You may recall that I said that the temporal tornado sucked in everything within two light-years. Krakar has to be fired at a distance of one point nine light-years from its target. So whoever fires it goes along with it. I suggest you draw straws or something and pick yourself a volunteer, quickly, while the rest of us get cheddite-projected back to the fleet."

There was a shuffling of feet, backward for the most part, since the desire to get trapped in a temporal tornado and whisked back to blow up and start the universe going did not seem to be a strong one.

But—there are some individuals who are big enough to face the idea of sacrifice for a cause, particularly for a cause as worthy as this one. These are the individuals who alter the destiny of worlds, and they are few and far between indeed. But when the need arises, they are ready to step forward, and step forward they do or the history of intelligence and civilization would not be where it is today.

Not one. Not two. But *three* stalwart figures stepped forward grimly, volunteering for certain death, volunteering to die so that the universe might live.

"One will be enough," Four said.

"Who will choose between us?" Jerry said, and John and Chuck smiled at this, and as one man, they put out their hands and clasped them together, comrades all.

"We will do it together," Chuck said. "It is our responsibility."

180

"The rest of you, go," John said. "It sure has been nice knowing you."

Quickly the Galaxy Rangers filed by, clasping the hands of their leaders in silence, knowing that this was the greatest day in the history of the galaxy. Many-eyed Slug-Togath shook a tentacular good-bye, web-fingered Pipa croaked his adieu with a tear in each large eye, Lord Prrsi soaked the tip of his great claw in ice water—ignoring the pain—so he too could have it shooken by them, while Troceps, clacking his great beak with emotion, shook hands as well and gave each of them one of his wing feathers for a souvenir. It was a heart-stopping, throat-choking moment. And as each Ranger stepped away, the cheddite projector whisked him back to the fleet which was already in full flight before the coming thunder of the temporal tornado. Number Four of the Chachkas was the last to go, and before he did, he injected a single note of hope.

"I make no guarantees, but you will remember I said that you will be caught up by the *edge* of the temporal tornado. There is no escaping from the heart of the storm, but at the edge, once you are in it, you may be able to re-wire Krakar to get you out. Maybe. No one of course knows, and it would take a genius to figure the thing out in time, but there you are. Even a billion-to-one odds chance, like this one, is better than no chance at all. So listen, say good-bye quick because I see the space armada, the greatest the universe has ever known, tearing down on you at top speed, so I have to go."

And he went, and the good companions were alone.

"Will you look at that!" Chuck said, and look they did indeed.

Space ahead was full, but *full*. Wall-to-wall spaceships. Ships such as had never been seen before away from the endless battle around Cotorra. Battleships that were twenty miles long and had gun turrets every eighty feet of their length. Ship after ship, fleet after fleet, squadron after squadron, all bearing down on the little shining form of the *Pleasantville Eagle*, every gun firing, every projector ravening rays, every torpedo zeroed in on *them*. Space was filled with hurtling death that rushed down on them with the force of destiny.

"You know," Chuck mused. "It makes you feel kind of humble."

"It makes me feel like pressing the goddamn button," Jerry said.

"Only three more light-years to go," added John.

"Well, you might have *told* me," Sally said, walking in with a great plate of salami sandwiches. "Here I've gone to all this trouble and everyone has left."

"I thought you went with the others!" John gasped. "And that you were crying too hard to say good-bye."

"Send her back with the cheddite projector!" Jerry shouted, diving for it.

"No time!" Chuck said, finger ready on the button. "One point nine light-years exactly . . . *now!*"

He pressed the button down savagely, and the can hissed slightly, and nothing else happened.

"It doesn't work!" more than one voice cried out, but more than one voice has been wrong before.

Because *something* was happening out there in interstellar space. Something that absorbed the energies of the ravening rays, rockets, shells, and torpedoes, eating them like candy, absorbing them into what can only be described as a black *hole* in the blackness of space, a new kind of blackness that hurt the eye to look upon. Beyond the *hole* the space armada sent out thousand-mile-long plumes of fire as they tried to brake and change course, but they could not. With frightening speed the black *hole* grew, absorbing them, eating them, growing larger all the time. Then, as the last great ship vanished, the blackness rushed out toward the *Pleasantville Eagle,* and Sally screamed at its terrible presence, and it was upon them.

For an unmeasurable instant time went mad. First it froze, and they were paralyzed and felt their hearts stop beating and the clocks stopped and even the molecules of matter stopped spinning. And then everything *reversed*. It is impossible to describe the sensation, except to say that it was not a nice one. They staggered, released suddenly

182

from the temporal paralysis, and it was Jerry who pointed out the front window and shouted, "Look!"

What a sight! Here at the rim of the temporal tornado it was relatively calm. Just an occasional bump when they ran over a minute or a clatter on the hull when they sailed through a cloud of seconds, nothing to bother over. But in the heart of the tornado it was a different matter! All the ships were being whirled about and buffeted together, glowing hotter and hotter as they did, already beginning to melt and run together into the primordial matter that would explode and form the universe.

"Might I ask just what is going on?" Sally asked.

"Let's get to work on the diagram," Jerry said, and an instant later he and Chuck were bent over the table scratching out equations. Therefore, it was John's unhappy duty to take Sally by the hand and take her aside and explain what had happened. She instantly burst out crying, and he let her weep upon his shoulder and stroked her smooth hair and made soothing noises. Soon her crying became a soft sobbing, and then she wiped her eyes and attempted a weak smile at him, and he smiled back and took a salami sandwich—he knew she would like that —then he took a second and a third and wolfed them down because this sort of thing gave him an appetite.

"Great sandwiches," he said, kindly.

"Thanks, John, I did my best." The little smile played across her tear-stained features and was as quickly gone. "But do we stand any chance at all of getting out of this thing?"

"Well, the odds are a billion to one, and those aren't what I call great betting odds. But Jerry and Chuck are geniuses, and if anyone can put Krakar into reverse gear and get us out of this, it is those two guys. Great guys."

"They are. And you are a great guy too."

"Aww, you're just saying that because it is the end of everything."

"Maybe, but one can't lie when everything is coming to an end? I feel honored to be loved by three such great guys as you three. Yes, John, I know, it was easy to tell,

183

there is no need to blush and turn away. You *are* blushing, aren't you? Yes, I thought so."

She took his great hand in her tiny one and squeezed just as Jerry jumped up shaking a piece of paper and shouted.

"Eureka!"

"What does that mean?" Sally gasped.

"I don't know, it's Greek. But we *have* it. Chuck did the math, and I have worked out a new circuit. Now, a bit of quick work with the old soldering iron, and we will see if the theory works."

He was as good as his word. They cannibalized some of the gunnery controls for spare parts, and within minutes he had breadboarded up a new circuit and opened up Krakar with a can opener and wired it into place.

"This is it," he said grimly, as he made delicate adjustments on the controls. "We will use the angular momentum of the tornado to hurl us backward in time and, since we are not going backward, that backward will really be forward, so we should be going in the right direction, back where we came from. After that it will just be a matter of cracking out of the time flow at the right place. All right, all set. Will you do the honors, Sally, darling? We foolishly got you into this, and let's see if your sweet finger will be the one to get us out of this. Press here."

She smiled at them all, blowing little kisses in their direction, then pushed delicately on the doorbell button that had been wired into the circuitry to actuate it.

Instantly everything went black. *Outside*, that is, but inside the plane it was as it was before, except everything seemed to move sluggishly, and it was an effort to do anything.

"Fighting . . . against . . . the current of time . . ." Jerry said, forcing the words from his lips. It was like moving through a sea of invisible molasses—but moving they were, for the time dial was slowly turning in reverse, and as it moved, faster and faster, their movements became easier until they were almost normal again.

"Wow!" Sally gasped, then sat down. "I don't want to have to go through that again!"

184

"You may have to when we get out," Chuck said, mumbling over some math. "There we go past one million *b.c.* Better get ready. Jerry, better adjust the frabbislator, see if we can come out near Earth."

"Right, it's done. Get ready, everyone—better strap in, because this might be the rough one."

Strap in they did, and the tension mounted as the needle spun. Back through the age of the giant saurians, the coming of the mammals, the emergence of man. Then Egypt, fiery Atlantis sinking, great Greece arising, a certain son of a carpenter born in Galilee, Roman orgies, bold King Arthur, the Dark Ages, the Magna Carta, knighthood in flower, the New World, the Industrial Revolution, pollution, world war, world war again, cold war, faster and faster and. . . .

"Now!" Jerry shouted and pressed.

With a sickening crunch the great 747 plunged through the time barrier and into the midnight sky of Earth. But the transition was not an easy one, for the time barrier is more solid than any sound barrier. Vibration racked the ship; equipment tore loose from its solid mooring; the right wing broke in half and hung, flapping, from a few remaining shards of metal. The left wing folded back over the plane with a horrifying crackling sound. The tail broke and almost fell off.

"Not bad," Chuck said, smiling. "We came through, and we're not dead yet. Where are we?"

"About thirty thousand feet up and falling fast," John said, tapping the altimeter. "I see lights down there, a city of some kind, and we're dropping right down on top of it."

"No point in trying to start the engines, is there?" Jerry laughed. "Not without any wings."

"No point at all," John agreed, looking out at the solid Earth that was rushing up toward them.

Sally screamed.

21

VICTORY WRENCHED FROM
THE SALIVATING JAWS
OF DEFEAT!

"Sally, Sally," Chuck said tenderly, patting her shoulder. "Now don't worry your pretty little head. We'll think of something. We have plenty of other gadgets aboard the ship. For instance the cheddite projector. . . ."

"Try again," Jerry said, picking up the bent and crushed projector from under a piece of heavy equipment that had fallen on it.

They tried, but it didn't seem to be much good. It was John who finally thought of the magnetic rays and who tore open the control case on the projector and exposed the interior wiring.

"Look, guys, if this is a magnetic attractor ray, why can't you reverse the thing and turn it into a magnetic deflector ray and stop our fall with it?"

"Twenty thousand feet up," Jerry said. "A great idea. Hand me a screwdriver, someone."

Tension filled the air while he sweated and worked.

"Ten thousand feet and falling fast," Chuck said to cheer him on, then ignored the viciously snarled answer.

"You know," John mused, looking out the window at the ground rushing up toward them, "I could be wrong, but that sure looks like Pleasantville down there."

"You are right," Sally gasped. "I can see the school, and my father's house, and there is the airport with a plane ready to take off."

"Five thousand feet," Chuck observed. "How does it look, old buddy?"

"One more connection—*there*. Strap in everyone."

They did, and at two thousand-feet altitude he pressed the button. The sudden deceleration hit them like a solid blow, and the fabric of the great plane screamed in protest. Things banged and crashed, and both wings fell off but remained hanging from the plane by pipes and cables and such, while the broken tail now fell off as well and hung in the same fashion. Deceleration grabbed them and crushed them, then eased up and vanished altogether.

"Phew," John said, "we're less than a thousand feet up and hovering."

"And right over the airport too. Hold it there a mo, Jerry, there is another plane taking off, going by right under us why . . . *look!*"

They looked—and gasped—for the other plane was the *Pleasantville Eagle!*

"I don't understand this," Sally said as the plane rushed by and was gone.

"Did you see who the pilot was?" John asked, shocked. "Why . . . it was *me!*"

"I think I know what has happened," Chuck said. "We timed our arrival back in our own time a little too precisely. So it looks like we have arrived back on Earth just before we originally took off. That is us going off, kidnapped by John."

"And the great adventure begins," Jerry said, looking after the great 747 now vanishing into the darkness. "If only we knew what we were getting into!"

"Don't tell us and ruin the fun!" John said, and they all laughed and the plane gave a sickening lurch and dropped.

"Wiring shorted!" Jerry cried, then labored over it.

Down they went, down and down, and they were just *feet* above the runway when he fixed it. He could slow their descent but not stop it and the plane crashed into the hard concrete with a horrendous crunch and instantly burst into flame.

"Save Sally!" someone shouted.

"I have her!" John called out, tearing her safety belt open and throwing her over one shoulder. "Take care of Chuck—he's been knocked cold!"

"I have him!" Jerry shouted, tearing open Chuck's safety belt in the same manner and shouldering his heavier burden. Thus laden, they staggered through the smoke-filled cabin to the exit ramp, which luckily had been jarred open by the crash and now reached down to the ground. Down it they went, with the flames licking at their very heels, and into a staggering run across the dew-wet grass. A welcome drainage ditch gaped before them, and even as they fell into it, the gallant old *Eagle* exploded with a roar of flame. And a crackle of shells as well, as all the ammunition went up.

"We made it!" Jerry gasped. "And what a grand show the old *Eagle* is making—what a way to go!"

The pyrotechnics lit up the entire sky and threw a flickering glow onto their faces as Sally opened her eyes.

"Safe," John said, simply, and in the instant she was in his arms, and their lips met, and they embraced. Sally liked to kiss with her eyes open, so she could see, over his strong shoulder, that Chuck had come to as well and that Jerry had taken *him* in his firm embrace and that they were kissing as well, passionately and long.

Since John and Sally had started first, they ran out of breath first, and their lips drew apart, but their arms still remained about each other as they sat and watched Jerry and Chuck slowly disengage. The two boys looked up and realized they were being watched, and, blushing, drew away from each other.

"No, that's all right," Sally said, smiling with understanding. "I've known for a long time that you both were AC-DC, and I was waiting for you to make your mind up which way you were finally going to jump. I know why you kept that cot in the laboratory." She laughed, and they laughed too and looked deep into each other's eyes and drew together again. "Not that I blame you, boys will be boys, and sometimes girls, but gee, that's what life is for. Loving I mean. In any case I have found the man I adore, and as soon as he asks me, we are going to be married."

"Marry me," John breathed.

"Yes, darling—just as soon as you grow a kinky beard and sideburns and a natural. Then you will look like you, and I will love you the more."

"Gee," John mused, "I don't know, darling. I had thought I would go down in the morning to the on-campus

188

branch of the friendly CIA and hit them up for a job. I bet they'll pay a lot for my specialized know-how and stuff."

"That is *not* the sort of work I would enjoy seeing any husband of mine doing," Sally replied coldly. "Leave that to the squares along with this mean-minded little town, and we will go to the big city and swing. Decide darling." She wriggled her hips deliciously and licked her full, moist lips while staring sensually from below half-lowered lids. "Me or the CIA . . . ?"

"Grr," he growled, pulling her unresisting body to his, his clawed fingers sinking deep into her fulsome rump. "A gold ring in my ear and more hair than you ever saw before."

"And you won't mind if I join fem lib and picket segregated male toilets and things? I've had about enough of the second-class citizen get-your-ass-back-into-the-kitchen you-poor-little-thing around here."

"Put that ring in my nose for all I care, honey. I am yours for life."

"That is very sweet of you to say, and I won't forget it, but will keep it sort of fifty-fifty if we can. And what about you guys?" she asked, turning to the other pair of unabashed lovers.

"Back to school," they said together, then burst out laughing.

"I have a couple of more degrees I need," Jerry said, "and I want to try out for the debating team."

"I have some more credits I need," Chuck added, "and I do really want to try out for the shot put. Can we room together, Jerry, honey?"

"Sure—I wouldn't have it any other way."

"Do you realize," John mused, looking at the flames of the burning 747 that were beginning to die down, "that it is as though it never happened."

"As though it were all a dream," Sally added.

"But it really happened," Jerry told them. "But it must be our secret. We can tell no one, or they would think us mad. We'll have to tell them that the ship crashed on takeoff."

"If the insurance won't cover a new plane, why, Dad will pay for it," Chuck said assuredly.

"Our secret," they said together, and joined hands, one over the other.

And then the Great Adventure really was over, and hand in hand, the two happy couples walked away across the dark field, walking into the future, heads high, knowing that they had been tried in the furnace of life and had emerged triumphant and well tempered to face anything that that future held in store.

A MIDSUMMER TEMPEST

Poul Anderson

'The best writing he's done in years ... his language is superb. Worth buying for your permanent collection.'
– *The Alien Critic*

Somewhere, spinning through another universe, is an Earth where a twist of fate, a revolution and a few early inventions have made a world quite unlike our own.

It is a world where Cavaliers and Puritans battle with the aid of observation balloons and steam trains; where Oberon and Titania join forces with King Arthur to resist the Industrial Revolution; and where the future meshes with the past in the shape of Valeria, time traveller from New York.

BEFORE THE GOLDEN AGE 3

Isaac Asimov

In this third volume, Isaac Asimov has selected a
feast of rousing tales such as BORN BY THE SUN
by Jack Williamson, with its marvellous vision of the
solar system as a giant incubator; Murray Leinster's
story of parallel time-tracks SIDEWISE IN TIME; and
Raymond Z. Gallin's OLD FAITHFUL which features
one of science fiction's most memorable aliens –
Number 774.

'Sheer nostalgic delight ... stories by authors
long-forgotten mingle with those by ones who are
well-known, and still writing. A goldmine for
anyone interested in the evolution of s.f.'
Sunday Times

'Contains some of the very best s.f. from the Thirties
... emphatically value for money.'
Evening Standard